Sign up for our newsletter to hear
about new and upcoming releases.

www.ylva-publishing.com

Other books in
The Midnight Coffee Series

Long-Distance Coffee
Coffee and Conclusions (Coming January 2018)

The Midnight Coffee Series Part One

Long-Distance Coffee

Emma Sterner-Radley

Dedication

This is for Swen.

Acknowledgments

First, I want to thank all the members of Swen for reading this story and, to my surprise, falling in love with it. You inspired it, fueled it, and made me believe I could be an author. This book wouldn't be here without you all!

Second, thank you to my amazing wife, Amanda, for saying, "Hey, why don't you try to write a romance? I bet you can if you really try." And for beta reading and supporting this romance she made me write.

I also need to thank Astrid and everyone at Ylva Publishing for wanting to publish it. Huge thanks to the editors who worked on this book, especially Andrea Bramhall. Andrea—thank you for going beyond being midwife and grandparent of this book by adding vodka aunt to the mix, too. You've poured a lot of your time and writing skills into this book, and I'm so grateful.

Before the professionals got their hands on it, two unpaid heroes helped out. Rebecca Fischer did a great job of beta reading and teaching me how things work in the US, while Eliana R. (5TenDays) helped with the Spanish phrases and checked that I got the references to Latinx culture right. Any mistakes that remain are solely mine (and were probably added after these two lovely ladies read the story.)

Additional thanks to HelveticaBrown for the song choice and to Lee Winter for the name of the FitWatch 9000.

This book needed you all.

Last but certainly not least, endless thanks to my long-suffering, loving family: Mamma, Pappa, Anna, Torbjörn, Oscar, Victor, and Ester. I hope you will see the sexy scenes coming and skip them. Or at least tell me you did. Seriously, it will make Christmas dinner a lot less awkward.

And, as always, in loving memory of
Malin Sterner
1973-2011
Jag saknar dig.

Chapter 1

Erin Black Can't Sleep

IT WAS LATE, AND SHE wished she had something to do. She picked off a strand of long, blonde hair that had stuck to her sweater. Erin prided herself on her hair, even though it wasn't very practical for a personal trainer who spent most of their time sweating in a gym.

She was standing by the window and moved her gaze out to the narrow, littered street below. It looked freezing out there, and it probably was. February in New York was always bitterly cold. Two middle-aged women staggered out from the Irish pub across the street and huddled together, as they laughed and stumbled their way down toward the avenue.

She sighed and turned around. The only light source in the dingy apartment was the bluish glow from her laptop standing on the table which served as both eating place and desk. Twitter was open. Erin had just started following an actor she had loved as a kid. It turned out that he was now a bitter old man, complaining about the lack of manners and the complacency of America's youth.

Erin sat down and scrolled through his timeline. Her bored expression moved a little toward interest, as she saw what had clearly been a dispute between the aging actor and someone who called themselves The_Apple_Core. Erin clicked *view conversation* to see what had been said. Apparently, her faded childhood hero had alleged women were too sensitive about jokes these days and seemed to think everything they didn't like was misogyny. The_Apple_Core had pointed out that they found that opinion to be misogynist and him to be "a washed-up embarrassment with the manners of a rhino."

Erin snorted out a laugh, which echoed though her quiet apartment.

The conversation between the two combatants continued, and Erin was impressed to see that, while her former childhood hero became more and more aggressive and insulting, his opponent did not. The_Apple_Core stuck to intelligent but snide remarks and made quite a few points about misogyny, respect, and seeing things from someone else's point of view. All of that was lost on the actor, but not on Erin. She clicked on the name and read the bio.

Sarcastic to the (apple) core. Mother of one. Writer. Latina. Moody. I live in Florida, and the sunshine and the cheerfulness is nearly killing me. Send help. And black coffee.

Erin smiled to herself as she clicked *follow*. She read through some of the tweets, some that made her laugh and some that made her think.

She looked at the button marked *Tweet to The_Apple_Core*. Had she been fully rested and in possession of the common sense that accompanied daylight, she probably wouldn't have clicked. But it was 12:52 p.m. on a Thursday night, and she knew that her insomnia was going to keep her up for at least another three to four hours, just like it had every other night for the last few months. She clicked and thought for a couple of moments about what to write.

> **@The_Apple_Core** Hey! I just wanted to thank you for explaining a few things to Dicky McActor earlier. I can't believe I had a T-shirt with his face on when I was 12!

She cursed loudly, as she realized it was too long. Damn Twitter and its 140-character limit. She started to fiddle with the message.

> **@The_Apple_Core** Wanted 2 thank you 4 explaining a few things to Dicky McActor. Can't believe I had a T-shirt with his face on when I was 12!

It wasn't Hemingway, but it would do. She rolled her shoulders and looked down at her mug of cold coffee. She got up to pour herself a hot refill from the full pot she always made before starting her long, wakeful nights.

Of course, she knew she shouldn't. Caffeine was sleep's worst enemy. But she'd tried everything to combat her sleeplessness: cutting out all caffeine, additional exercise, better diet, herbal teas of all kinds, relaxation techniques, meditation, massage…even going to a doctor. So far, the only thing that helped was heavy sleeping pills, and they made her feel numb and drowsy the following day. She'd rather be tired and cranky than walk into walls and be spacey all day. So, yeah, she allowed herself the caffeine. If she had to be up, she might as well be feeling human throughout the night.

She took a sip of the strong brew. The little heat sting on her lips was nothing compared with how the acidic liquid was going to burn her stomach lining. She was usually very health conscious, she had to be as a personal trainer—so she felt she could allow herself one little, body-torturing vice.

Her laptop made a muted little noise. She always kept the sound low so as not to bother the neighbors. She walked over to check her e-mails and found a Twitter notification. The_Apple_Core had replied.

Erin gave a surprised little "huh," before remembering that Florida was in the same time zone as New York and that it wasn't *that* late there. Still, it was a bit late for a mom to be up. Maybe not so late for a writer. Didn't those creative people keep weird hours? She clicked the Twitter link and read.

@BuffBlonde83 He needed a long cold-facts-and-common-sense shower. I'm sure he didn't even grasp half of it, though.

Erin smiled again and bit her lower lip, as she considered her reply.

@The_Apple_Core Probably not. But hopefully, some of his followers did. Maybe you made a current 12-year-old throw HER T-shirt away.

A reply came in quickly. Clearly this writer chick was quick at typing.

@BuffBlonde83 I don't care about their apparel, but if I made them think for themselves, then I am proud of my work here tonight.

3

Keen to keep up the same pace and carry on the conversation, Erin didn't think twice before answering.

> **@The_Apple_Core** You should be! If not because you educated the kids, then because you smacking that asshole down really made my night. ;-)

It was only after she had clicked send that she realized this reply might seem a little too…flirty? "You made my night." And then the winking smiley. Was that okay to say to a stranger online? Shit. Could she not be such a huge gay for two seconds and have a conversation with a woman without borderline flirting?

The next reply took longer to come in. Erin sighed before rolling her shoulders again. She had just resigned herself to deciding she had been too friendly, too fast and had scared her conversation partner off.

> **@BuffBlonde83** Then my night hasn't been wasted. Speaking of nights, shouldn't you be asleep?

With a smile, Erin quickly typed back.

> **@The_Apple_Core** Yeah, I have work tomorrow morning, so I should. But insomnia is a bitch and has me totally whipped. Why are you up?

There was a moment's pause during which Erin ran her hand through her tousled blonde hair.

> **@BuffBlonde83** Sleep is a luxury for people without babies. Mine wakes every two hours. I might as well be awake and nap with him tomorrow.

Erin whistled low to herself, happy that she'd decided against having kids. Not that anyone had ever offered to have them with her. Most of her girlfriends hadn't stuck around long enough for the topic to even come up.

> **@The_Apple_Core** Ouch! I know some kids don't sleep, but he sounds like a bad case. Is he an insomniac like me?

There was a long break again, and Erin wondered if she had done her usual trick of putting her foot in it. Had she sounded like she was criticizing the kid?

> **@BuffBlonde83** No, not really. However, I'm sure that anyone not knee-deep in the world of babies would be bored with hearing the details.

Erin tilted her head and thought. She knew nothing about babies. But she was bored stiff, and this woman seemed interesting. She could always bail if the baby talk got dull.

> **@The_Apple_Core** I can't sleep, and I'm tired of watching TV or scrolling through Twitter. Try me.

> **@BuffBlonde83** Fine. Don't say I didn't warn you. He has problems with his tummy & the pain wakes him. The doctor said he will grow out of it.

Erin swallowed a mouthful of coffee before replying.

> **@The_Apple_Core** Poor little dude! Think it's stress related? Has he got a lot to do at work? Bills to pay?

As soon as she pressed *Tweet*, Erin wondered if her joke would go over well. What if this woman thought she was mocking her son's pain and lack of sleep? The reply took a while, and Erin wondered if she was more invested in this chat to a stranger than she ought to be. *Shit, I must be getting lonely*, she thought. Finally, her laptop quietly pinged.

> **@BuffBlonde83** I don't know. Does that usually cause intestinal gas and sometimes vomiting up your milk?

Erin snorted into the coffee she was drinking.

> **@The_Apple_Core** Wouldn't know, never had an ulcer. Maybe he should cut down on the coffee? ;-)

> **@BuffBlonde83** The only coffee he gets is from my milk. I only allow myself two small cups a day, though, to limit the caffeine transfer.

5

Erin blinked a couple of times. *Whoa, we're actually talking about her breast milk? This chick's certainly not shy,* she mused. Before Erin had time to reply, there was another tweet.

> **@BuffBlonde83** I suppose you are now going to lecture me on drinking coffee while breastfeeding and about keeping a healthy diet?

Erin saw the defensiveness and chuckled. People always assumed that because of her profession she would judge their eating habits and their exercise regime, or lack thereof. The truth was that Erin knew what people should do, but as she did not always do so herself, she tried not to throw stones from inside her glass house.

> **@The_Apple_Core** I don't judge. And, anyway, I couldn't live without coffee, so I don't blame you. Plus, you'll get him into coffee early. Kudos!

> **@BuffBlonde83** Oh, thank God. I couldn't stand another lecture on what to do with my non-sleeping baby right now. Are you a coffee fan too?

Erin looked down at her now empty coffee mug.

> **@The_Apple_Core** Yeah, against my own advice, I drink buckets of the stuff. It's probably gonna kill me one day.

> **@BuffBlonde83** We all have to die somehow. There are worse poisons. I hear moms complaining about giving up alcohol, but that was easy for me.

Another tweet came in right away, and Erin was again impressed by how fast this woman typed, not to mention the lack of typos.

> **@BuffBlonde83** So was giving up the seafood and other foodstuffs that are bad during pregnancy and breastfeeding. But coffee is a must.

Erin wondered why this mom was so defensive. Was it because she was—according to her Twitter bio—a first-time mom, or was it just in her personality?

@The_Apple_Core It sounds like you are doing fine, but I know nothing about kids. What kind of coffee do you like?

Erin was expecting a brand she knew, as she had tried every kind available in her local grocery store. She had even gone down to an organic, fair-trade shop to buy really pricey coffee, which in the end, tasted like crap.

@BuffBlonde83 It's called Azúcar Negra. The coffee beans are dried and stored with burnt sugar & take up the taste from that. That's the theory anyway.

Erin frowned, as she typed out a reply.

@The_Apple_Core Never heard of it. Some kinda exotic import stuff?

@BuffBlonde83 Afraid so. Call me pretentious, but it tastes amazing, and when you can only have a little, you certainly want those cups to count.

Erin grinned, unable to resist taking the bait.

@The_Apple_Core Okay, you're pretentious. ;-) Makes sense, tho. Where'd you get it?

@BuffBlonde83 I order it online, and it ships from Guatemala. It's pricey but certainly worth it for the small quantities I have.

Erin shook her head and looked over at her coffee pot and its dark liquid.

@The_Apple_Core Well, living on my salary and forking out for a New York apartment means I don't have money to burn. I'm sticking to Maxwell House.

@BuffBlonde83 Your loss. I have to go. Little Alberto seems to be waking up, and he'll need me to walk around with him for a while.

Erin was disappointed. This Apple Core person was really making time go by faster. She felt guilty resenting the baby for waking up and ending the conversation early.

@The_Apple_Core Okay. Thanks for the chat. Good night and good luck with the lil' stressed-out man.

There was no reply, but that was to be expected if her new acquaintance had rushed off to pick up a screaming baby. Erin rubbed her eyes, realizing a moment too late that she hadn't removed her mascara and now probably looked like a panda.

She cursed under her breath and went to wash off her makeup. After that, she figured she would have to spend her upcoming sleepless hours with the TV on. Or perhaps she could watch some puppy videos YouTube. *Or maybe google that weird-ass coffee that sits around in burnt sugar,* she thought to herself, as she turned on the bathroom tap.

Chapter 2

Isabella Martinez Can't Sleep

It was ten thirty at night, and the house was finally silent. Only Isabella was awake. She wished that wasn't the case, though.

She sat under a blanket in the plush armchair she'd put in the nursery. It was comfortable for long nights of snoozing, using her relatively new iPad, and rocking a fussing baby back to sleep.

She blinked her tired eyes and looked around. The small room was her and Alberto's own safe little world. Everything smelled of Alberto and baby powder, to the point where Isabella wondered if her perfume was even detectable on her skin anymore. It didn't matter to her, though.

At night, all that mattered was that she and Alberto both got as many moments of sleep as they could. The rest of the time, she was supposed to do housework or write. After all, she'd abandoned a lucrative career as CEO for a large catering company with franchises all over the nation for motherhood. Not that she missed her former occupation. Not really. She missed the daily social interaction, and she missed the adrenaline rush of power, even though that last thought left a bad taste in her mouth. She had never thought of herself as power hungry. That title belonged to her mother. But, yes, there had always been a certain high in being admired, being obeyed, and having the power to change things as she saw fit.

Is that how Mother feels? Is that why she does what she does? To get that rush?

She shook her head. That wasn't the point here.

The point was that she had given it all up to have Alberto and write her novel about retellings of fairy tales, so that was what she was going to do. Even if it killed her. She had to prove she could. She had to prove to her mother that she had made the right decision.

In her mind, she heard her mother's derisive voice mocking her wish to write. She closed her eyes tightly to rid herself of the unwanted memory.

There was a noise from the crib next to her—a little, muffled baby grunt. She waited. But, no, Alberto didn't wake up this time. He just gave a little sigh before returning to soft, deep breaths. She relaxed and looked back to the iPad screen, which she'd turned down as dark as it could go and still be legible.

She was supposed to be writing. What she was actually doing was checking out the Twitter profile that began "Erin Black—Personal Trainer."

It was an odd thing for her to be doing, as she very rarely spent her sleepless nights speaking to people. Talking to people online late at night could lead to trouble, as the people who were up weren't always reasonable or appreciative of her wry brand of humor. But last night's brief exchange had been diverting. It had been nice to discuss Alberto's problems with a complete outsider. She hadn't judged, given advice that Isabella had heard a million times, asked stupid questions, or generally annoyed her.

That was rare. Most people managed to push Isabella's buttons and get her snapping at them in seconds, leaving them disliking her and Isabella berating herself. She didn't know why she did it. Well, actually she did. Her mother was famous for snapping at people and being unnecessarily harsh. Of all the things to inherit from her mother, she had to get that undesirable trait.

Alberto moved again, and Isabella watched him, only to see that it was another false alarm. Thankfully, he seemed quite deep in sleep tonight. She knew that she should probably turn the iPad off and try for a few hours' sleep too.

Soon. She just had to check what this Erin Black was talking about with someone who called themselves RedHeadRedHot, which sounded terribly like something from a porno. Not that Isabella had watched one of those since she was in her early twenties. She wondered if they'd gotten more tasteful since then. She sincerely doubted it.

She brought her focus back to the conversation on Twitter and a tweet from Erin.

@RedHeadRedHot Are you actually going to show tomorrow, or will I be at the gym with my weights, looking like I was stood up for a date AGAIN?

@BuffBlonde83 Chill, woman. I paid for the session, so I'll be there. I was just hungover and forgot last time. You gonna go easy on me, Er?

@RedHeadRedHot Stop calling me Er, Riley. It's weird. Oh, and hell no, so I recommend you don't show up hungover this time.

@BuffBlonde83 Wanna make me sweat, huh? I knew you were into me. ;-)

@RedHeadRedHot Ha! Just coz I'm into women and nice to you doesn't mean I want to bang you, Riley.

A second tweet from Erin followed right after it.

@RedHeadRedHot Oh, and stop outing me on Twitter, or get yourself a new personal trainer! :-P

@BuffBlonde83 Dude. Your bio says you are Out & Proud. YOU outed you, Er. I just spoke the truth about what you really want—ME!

Isabella realized she was frowning. She wasn't sure if it was the pet name for Erin, the way the person spoke, or something else, but she wasn't a fan of this Riley. She scrolled farther, seeing what Erin had replied.

@RedHeadRedHot It did say that when you met me. It doesn't anymore, dumbass.

@BuffBlonde83 Oh shit! I didn't realize. I'm really sorry, Er. Want me to remove the tweet?

@RedHeadRedHot Nah, it's fine. If people don't want a gay trainer, they can just pick someone else. I have no need to train homophobes anyway.

@BuffBlonde83 It would be their loss, babe. Well, I can't sit around here. New York is full of hot people to meet and Mama wants some fun. BYEEEE!

@RedHeadRedHot At the risk of sounding like your mom, be safe, have fun, and don't be too hungover for our session tomorrow!

@BuffBlonde83 Yeah, whatevs. If you can't sleep, I recommend a hot bath and then rubbing one out. Always works for me! ;-)

@RedHeadRedHot Fuck, Riley! Inappropriate much? Go get laid. I'm gonna have coffee and stalk my ex on Facebook. Like a civilized person!

The conversation ended there. Isabella realized that her eyebrows had shot up at some of the stuff she had read. Firstly, because all of that had been said on a public forum where anyone could see, and secondly, because her new Twitter friend was a lesbian. Interesting. The joke about stalking an ex… So, she was single. None of this mattered in any way, of course. It was just plain curiosity on Isabella's side.

Alberto kicked his little white-and-blue-onesie-clad foot at the side of the crib. Isabella put her hand over the bars and gently rubbed the spot to make sure the pain didn't wake him. His foot was soft, and she could feel the tiny toes move as she hummed quietly to soothe him. It didn't work. His eyes opened, and he gave a heart-wrenching cry.

She picked Alberto up and cradled him to her chest while rubbing his back. She shushed him softly and hummed his favorite lullaby. He kept screaming but a little less urgently now. Soon, he settled and kept to little coughing sobs and whines.

She kept rubbing his back and rocking him, as she walked over to the window. He seemed to like looking out at the starry night when he woke. Although, Isabella wondered how much his baby eyes could focus on. She kept humming and kissed his downy head. He gurgled unhappily but otherwise stayed quiet.

Isabella could see Richard's car outside, parked badly on their drive. As always. That man could never park straight, and it bothered Isabella. Everything about him bothered her lately. She felt like such a bitch. Sometimes, she wondered if she didn't mind being cooped up in this little room with Alberto all night, because it meant being far away from Richard. Without having to justify her absence. What father would begrudge her the care of their infant?

In here, she didn't have to listen to Richard snoring all night long. Or be surrounded by his mugs of herbal tea strewn around their bedroom, the dregs of which tainted the air with their distinctive aroma. She didn't have to sleep in bedclothes that smelled of the outdoors and that annoying cologne he always wore. Or put up with his mud-caked clothes thrown on the floor until he ran out of things to wear and had to wash them. Although if she was honest, she would usually tire of the stench of the dirt and swamp water before then and wash them for him. And of course, she didn't have to wake up with an erection pressed against her back.

She regretted the unkind thoughts the moment they entered her mind. He was Alberto's father; he was a good man, and she was the one who had decided that they should give a relationship a go. She just wished that he—her eyes focused back on the car—could park properly.

Alberto nuzzled at her shoulder, and she realized he was looking for food. She sat down in the armchair, unbuttoned her shirt, and started to feed him. She looked down at the iPad she'd abandoned on the side table. Erin Black's Twitter feed looked up at her, and she used her free hand to scroll up to the bio.

The blonde woman in profile was wearing aviator sunglasses. From what Isabella could see in the little picture, Erin looked attractive. Under the picture was a brief introduction.

I'm Erin Black. I'm a New Yorker and a personal trainer who's very friendly at work but really a loner. I can't sleep (like, ever), and I can't stand racists/ homophobes/misogynists. My landlord won't let me have a dog, and that pisses me off daily.

While Alberto ate, Isabella scrolled down Erin Black's Twitter feed. Most of it was retweets about dogs, TV shows, and physical fitness. There were a few personal tweets, mostly about if it was snowing or not, and how little she was sleeping.

As Isabella scrolled, she saw new tweets. *Erin must have decided against stalking her ex, or perhaps she was joking about that.*

She shifted in the armchair to make herself and Alberto more comfortable and to make it easier for her to use her free hand to scroll up on the iPad. She quickly clicked to *Follow* Erin Black's profile, telling herself that she could always unfollow her if this woman turned out to be annoying. She read the new tweet.

> Dammit. I'm really bored, and my coffee sucks because I put too much water in. Distract me, Twitter!

Isabella smiled, ever so slightly, and noticed that Alberto had fallen back asleep. She put the iPad down, gently placed Alberto back in his crib, and tucked him in.

She buttoned up, cursing under her breath when she saw a few drops of milk on her pajama shirt, and then sat back down in the armchair. She got the iPad and quietly tapped out a reply to BuffBlonde83.

Chapter 3

The Second Night of Tweeting

ERIN WAS PUTTING HER STILL-DAMP hair up in a ponytail when the laptop beeped. She walked over. It was The_Apple_Core. She punched the air and shouted, "Yes." She'd included the coffee reference as a little shout-out to the Floridian writer. She hadn't dared hope it would work, though.

She needed to talk to someone interesting, since she had just been caught on Facebook by a former client who wanted to talk about her brother-in-law's bad back and ask what Erin would recommend. Erin hated being forced into conversations; it made her feel panicked and weirdly exhausted afterward. Sharing a few tweets with The_Apple_Core was different, though. It was relaxing and fun. At least it had been last night. She hurried to read the reply to her own tweet.

> **@BuffBlonde83** Too much water? Sounds like someone was too tired to make coffee tonight. Tut-tut. It's not even midnight yet.

Erin chuckled before replying.

> **@The_Apple_Core** I know, right? I had just gotten out of the shower, so maybe I was preoccupied, but still...need to make another pot.

> **@BuffBlonde83** Yes, or you won't be able to stay up and see the wonders of late-night Twitter. Especially the spirited "debates."

Erin sat down, pulling the towel she was wearing down a bit to protect her from the cold seat of her chair.

@The_Apple_Core Gah! Don't even get me started on that. I stay in my lane as long as ppl don't say anything offensive.

@BuffBlonde83 But then you step in?

Erin nodded while she typed the reply.

@The_Apple_Core Hell yeah. Someone has to put a stop to that sort of thing.

@BuffBlonde83 Erin Black—the savior of Twitter. You just need some armor and a sword.

Erin sat up and frowned in puzzlement for a moment. How did this woman know her name? Taking a breath, she remembered that it was in her Twitter bio and focused on writing a response.

@The_Apple_Core Nah! I just don't like injustice and people treating other people like crap. Society is tough enough without people being assholes, y'know?

@BuffBlonde83 Colorful language there. But I certainly agree with the sentiment.

@The_Apple_Core I know you do! I saw what you did to a certain actor yesterday, remember?

Erin sat back and waited for a reply. Time ticked by, and while other tweets popped up all around her, there were no replies from The_Apple_Core.

The small apartment smelled of her strawberry shampoo and conditioner. Erin greedily inhaled the fresh, sweet scent and made a mental note to buy more of that brand. She stretched a bit. Still no reply.

She went to make a fresh pot of coffee, making damn sure she got the correct coffee-to-water ratio this time. She was contemplating putting some music on when the quiet beep of the laptop rang out. She flicked the switch to turn on the coffeemaker and hurried back to the laptop.

@BuffBlonde83 Sorry. Alberto (my son) woke up, and I had to walk around with him until his stomach settled and he fell back asleep.

@The_Apple_Core No probs. I was just remaking the coffee. Did you two have a nice walk?

@BuffBlonde83 No, not really. His room is far too small for anything more than a walk to the window and then back again.

Erin picked up a protein bar and ripped open the top of the packaging with her teeth.

@The_Apple_Core You can't take him into your bedroom and have him in your bed?

This time there was a longer pause before the reply came in.

@BuffBlonde83 No, he has to stay in his room so his crying doesn't wake his dad. Richard has to be up at 6 and get to work. So we stay in here.

Erin read the reply. Twice. She wondered why she felt so disappointed. Was it because the world sometimes seemed so filled with straights, and she longed to talk to people like her? She chastised herself for her assumption. Living with a man didn't make this woman heterosexual; she could be bi— or pansexual even.

Erin shook off the unwanted disappointment. After all, she was just whiling away some time by talking to a stranger who lived about a million miles away, some rich chick with a kid and a husband who could afford expensive coffee. Most likely, they didn't have anything in common and would probably not even become friends. What did it matter if this woman was in a steady relationship and into guys?

She typed out a reply and sent it before going to get the coffee which had now finished brewing.

@The_Apple_Core Ah, Okay. What does your husband do? (If you don't mind me asking.)

@BuffBlonde83 We're not married. He runs a charity that focuses on saving the endangered wildlife here in Florida.

Another tweet came in right afterward.

@BuffBlonde83 He's out wading through swamps or in offices schmoozing patrons all day, so he needs his sleep.

Erin returned to her laptop and knitted her brows, as she decided what to reply.

@The_Apple_Core What about you? Don't you need sleep to be a writer?

There was another long pause, and Erin felt sure that she had blown it and asked too many questions. She worried that she'd offended The_Apple_Core or made her feel bad about her situation. She sighed and muttered, "Damn it, Black, you should have just made a joke about dredging through swamps being good leg exercise."

Finally, a reply popped up.

@BuffBlonde83 Not as much as Richard needs it. I write between naps both in the daytime and at night. It works perfectly well, thank you.

Erin winced. There was the sarcasm, or maybe it was the moodiness that Apple Core's Twitter profile warned about.

@The_Apple_Core Right, of course. I didn't mean to question your setup there. Just curious and bad at, like, phrasing stuff, you know?

Another pause. Erin realized she was holding her breath.

@BuffBlonde83 I understand. Sorry if I seemed defensive. I've been told that I tend to come off as rather snappy.

Erin smiled, relieved that the conversation was back on track. She took another bite of her protein bar.

@The_Apple_Core That explains why your bio says you are moody and sarcastic to the (apple) core. I like your Twitter handle btw.

@BuffBlonde83 Thank you. I've been fond of apples ever since I was a little girl, and, well, coming up with these names can be tricky.

> **@The_Apple_Core** Hey, mine is not exactly Shakespeare material. ;)

> **@BuffBlonde83** To be honest, I am surprised yours doesn't involve dogs. You seem to be a big canine fan.

> **@The_Apple_Core** Ah, you've seen my tweets then, huh? Yeah, love dogs. Always wanted one as a kid, but foster homes don't really allow it.

There was another lengthy pause, and Erin wondered if the reference to her past had put the other woman off, or if the kid had woken up again.

She was aware that some people shied away from a sob story, especially if they were just trying to kill some hours online by mindlessly chatting to a stranger. She wasn't looking for sympathy or getting ready to pour her heart out. Erin had accepted her past and moved on, but this Apple Core person couldn't know that. Maybe she wondered why Erin would tweet about it in public.

Erin took a long swig of coffee and grimaced as the still-too-hot liquid stung in her mouth and throat. A tweet came up on her screen.

> **@BuffBlonde83** Sorry, Alberto needed to be changed. Sorry you weren't allowed a dog. I read in your bio that you can't have 1 now either?

Before Erin had time to reply, there was another tweet from The_Apple_Core.

> **@BuffBlonde83** I can't believe I just had to put a numeral into that sentence instead of typing out one. Sometimes I hate Twitter and its 140 characters.

Erin couldn't help smirking at that comment. It was clear that Apple Core liked to speak and write properly. She was either really obsessed about her language use or just educated out the wazoo. Erin made a mental note to find out which it was.

She looked at the tweet again and realized that there was an opportunity to take the public conversation to a more private platform. She wondered if her new chat partner would go for it.

After a moment of pondering, she came up with a jokey comment. Apple Core could easily shoot it down without it seeming harsh.

> **@The_Apple_Core** :D If you use Facetime or Skype, we could chat there? I can tell u about my lack of puppy goodness in 50,000 chars!

> **@BuffBlonde83** I wouldn't know what Facetime was even if it was staring me straight in the face. I have a rarely used Skype account, though.

> **@The_Apple_Core** Cool! DM me your Skype user name, and I'll add you.

Erin smiled. Her gamble had paid off. She anxiously waited for the next message. It was, however, taking longer than she had expected, and she picked up her coffee again.

> **@BuffBlonde83** All right. I give up. What is a DM? (Don't mock me, or I'll make you regret it!)

Erin snorted a laugh into her coffee.

> **@The_Apple_Core** Dog Mole. :D It's a direct message (private) here on Twitter. Just so no one else here can see your username and try to add you.

There was another pause during which Erin giggled at her Dog Mole joke. Then her Twitter account informed her that she had a DM. She opened it and read.

> *I think you might have been mocking me and my technophobic ways, but as I'm not sure, you may live. I've had a look and my username appears to be IsabellaMartinez1.*

Erin put her coffee down and typed enthusiastically. For some reason, it made her excited to find out the woman's name. She stopped typing and bit her lip. What if Isabella Martinez was a writer or painter or something, and she was just too uncultured to have heard of her? Should she take a chance and risk sounding dumb?

Yeah, she decided to risk it. If she was wrong and this chick mocked her, at least she'd know what kind of person she was dealing with and avoid her—unless the mocking was funny, of course. She continued typing and clicked send.

Cool. Hey, does that mean I know your name now? I've never known anyone called Isabella. It's an awesome name, btw. (Don't worry, I'm not a stalker or so lonely I'd be likely to become obsessed with you or anything… much. ;-))

The reply came in, and its contents made Erin's tense shoulders relax.

Yes, that's me. Isabella Martinez. I was named after Isabela, the Puerto Rican municipality that my grandfather came from before he emigrated to the US. I actually wasn't worried about you being a stalker until you said that. Thanks for putting that unpleasant thought in my head.

Erin grinned as she answered.

I'm as normal as anyone who sits up and drinks coffee all night can be. :-P You'll get an "add me" message on Skype from BlackVelvetBitches. (It was funny when I signed up, like, ten years ago. You know, because my last name is Black. Never mind.)

The reply pinged in, and Erin nearly missed it because she was busy looking down, trying to shake her embarrassment.

I'm not a fan of the use of the word "bitches," but I like the rest. Is it from the song? "Black Velvet?"

Erin had to answer that right away.

Yes! Not everyone gets that reference. I loved that song. Well…I still kinda do.

Isabella's answer came just as quickly as Erin's had.

It's a good song.

A thrill rushed through Erin's system. She hadn't felt like this while talking to someone for a very long time. She forced herself to focus on typing a reply.

*Yep. I like your Twitter handle too. What's with the apple thing? You said
you liked them since you were a kid?*

Erin realized that this might be a long story. She wondered if she should
have waited until they were typing in the much-easier Skype chat? The
reply proved to be quite short, luckily.

*I used to have a huge apple tree outside my window when I was a child.
It became a sort of symbol for me, I suppose. And I have always liked the
taste and smell of apples.*

Erin stopped herself from saying that she liked apples too but mainly if
they were in a pie or a protein flapjack. Would that be interesting? Would
it make her sound like a bad personal trainer if she admitted to not liking
the fruit raw? She had to stop second-guessing everything. *This is why you
don't socialize, Black*, she thought to herself. She stuck to using her reply to
move the chat.

Gotcha. Okay, I'll see you on Skype.

Erin opened the app and thought about what she could talk about
to prove that she was smart, funny, and totally normal to this Isabella
Martinez. Next to Erin, her forgotten coffee was going cold, while she was
just getting warmed up.

Chapter 4

Skype

ISABELLA SUDDENLY FELT WORRIED. SHE started wondering if they were supposed to be typing to each other, as she had assumed, or if they were supposed to be calling each other over Skype.

She shook her head and decided that this Erin Black would know that voices would wake Alberto and that she didn't seem forward enough just to call without asking first.

Erin seemed quite sensible and easygoing. That was one of the reasons it was nice to talk to her. She hoped they would keep the conversation flowing easily. The last thing she wanted was to become annoyed and say something rude to her new acquaintance. Especially in her sleep-deprived state. If she was honest with herself, she was simply too tired to censor herself; this woman would just have to take her as she was. But Isabella was eager for this conversation to flow easily—as easily as all the previous interactions had been with Erin. *Stop overthinking. I simply need to be myself and let the conversation develop as it will.*

The Skype app on her iPad showed her the request from BlackVelvetBitches. She accepted and opened a chat window.

> **IsabellaMartinez1:** Hello. Before we start any conversation, I would like to ask you to refrain from telling me about your lack of "puppy goodness" in 50,000 characters. I'm sure you can limit yourself to a few thousand.

A little pen and the words, BlackVelvetBitches is typing…appeared at the bottom of the window.

> **BlackVelvetBitches:** God, demanding much? :D Okay, so, yeah, I don't have a dog, but I'd love one. Someone to go running with and someone to cuddle up with at night. Someone loyal. Who won't leave, you know? Who's just always there and happy to see you.

Isabella read the words carefully. She felt that there was more in those sentences than just the wish for a dog. *Someone loyal. Who won't leave, you know?* That sounded like Erin had known a lot of people who weren't.

Isabella sighed. Her tired brain was probably overthinking again. The woman just wanted a dog, for heaven's sake.

The rustle of a moving blanket made her look over at the sleeping baby in his little crib. Alberto stopped moving, made a little snuffling sound in his sleep, and then grew quiet again.

That phrase popped into her mind again; *who's just always there and happy to see you.* Isabella realized she had that. No matter what was happening in her life, whether she had another setback with her writing, a quarrel with her mother, or another disappointing encounter with Richard, Alberto was always there, and if not happy, at least comforted to see her.

Alberto liked being picked up by his dad, and being cuddled or played with by other people, but at the end of the day, she was the only one who could comfort him. The only one he was always "happy" to see. She shook herself out of her reverie and went back to her iPad.

> **IsabellaMartinez1:** In a way, I have that with Alberto. Minus the going out running, of course. Although, we do go for long walks with him in the stroller. So, yes, I understand what you mean. Would your landlord let you have a smaller animal? A rabbit or perhaps a guinea pig?

The little pen appeared immediately, and Isabella felt strangely proud that the other woman was so interested in their conversation that she hadn't tabbed out or left the screen while Isabella had been lost in thought.

> **BlackVelvetBitches:** Nope. No pets allowed. I'm not gonna complain, though, getting an apartment in this part of town without cockroaches is awesome.

Isabella smiled.

> **IsabellaMartinez1:** Surely it would be better if there were cockroaches? Then you could have them as pets? I hear they're quite loyal and they can certainly run fast, so they would be great jogging partners.

> **BlackVelvetBitches:** Yeah, they run fast. But always in the opposite direction. Besides, I doubt I could housebreak them. You're a mom, you should know... Do they make diapers in cockroach sizes?

She chuckled at the mental image of a cockroach in a diaper. She glanced at her son for a moment, worried her laughter had woken him. Alberto's arms and legs moved fervently, showing that he was probably dreaming something intense, but he didn't wake. Isabella looked back at her iPad and typed.

> **IsabellaMartinez1:** Hmm. Perhaps newborn swaddling diapers could work for the bigger cockroaches? Otherwise, I'm afraid you'll have to make your own out of cloth.

Isabella had just hit *send* when she looked at the message. She frowned and scrunched up her nose. This was a ridiculous discussion. She had to pull this back to something sensible. She typed another message.

> **IsabellaMartinez1:** So, what is it like being a PT?

BlackVelvetBitches took a while to reply. Isabella saw the pen appear but it took a long time before she saw a message.

> **BlackVelvetBitches:** Sorry, I went to get a refill on the coffee. I have to start by saying that I try to call myself a personal trainer and not a PT. Physical therapists use the letters PT, and they REALLY don't want any confusion. My job is great on good days

and awful on bad days. But I guess that is pretty much all jobs, huh? *shrug*

Isabella began typing fast, not even caring about the issues with autocorrect. Despite having had the iPad for over a month, she still hadn't gotten over the thrill of the device. Her fingers on the screen made a lot less noise than a keyboard, which made it less likely that Alberto would wake up as she worked, or chatted, in this case. That alone was worth the frustration of autocorrect and slower typing.

IsabellaMartinez1: You might have a point there. What does a bad day look like for a personal trainer?

Another brief pause and Isabella wondered if Erin was sipping. It gave her a craving for the rich, sharp flavor of coffee. She'd only had one cup today. Maybe she should have her second one soon. She decided to go downstairs and get one the next time Alberto woke up.

BlackVelvetBitches: It could be a lot of things, like a lot of appointments back-to-back, which makes it stressful, or a client who is difficult in some way. Or I could just be having a bad day, physically or mentally.

Isabella's interest was piqued, the coffee craving forgotten for now.

IsabellaMartinez1: Physically or mentally? How do you mean?

BlackVelvetBitches: Physically, as in I could have a cold or could have pulled a muscle but still have to show the regime I've set up for the client. Mentally, as in that I might not be in the mood to socialize.

Isabella sat up straighter in her chair.

IsabellaMartinez1: Ah, is this the famous loner trait you mentioned in your Twitter bio?

BlackVelvetBitches: Depends. Are you asking as someone making friends or as a writer studying people? ;-)

IsabellaMartinez1: Ha. All right, you caught me. A little of both, I suppose. I'm always curious when someone says they're a loner. It makes me wonder if they mean they're antisocial, introverted, or just very comfortable being alone. Or a combination of those traits.

BlackVelvetBitches: Hmm, well. I don't dislike people. I really like a few, actually. :-P I just get really tired and freaked out when I've done too much socializing. It's a real pain with my job. I have to make small talk and try to make the clients like me, and it makes me kinda edgy, you know? I hate to be rude to people, but sometimes I just want them to go away and let me work out or read my comics in peace. Weird, huh?

IsabellaMartinez1: I wouldn't say so. In fact, that sounds to me like you'd fit perfectly in the introvert category. A lot of people are introverts. There's nothing wrong with that at all.

BlackVelvetBitches: Whoa, look at you analyzing me! I better not find myself in a book somewhere as the INTROVERT and weird Twitter stalker who likes dogs and coffee. I'll be watching out for myself in your books, Martinez!

Isabella paused and ran her hand over the back of her neck. Her fingers snagged in her thick hair, and she was momentarily distracted, wondering if she should cut her hair or not. But reality pulled her back down into her unpleasant thoughts and having to reply to Erin. Her books. Right.

IsabellaMartinez1: I write about fairy tales, so you should be safe. Anyway, the way my writing is going, I doubt you'll ever find any books in the first place.

She almost regretted the admission as soon as she sent it. She hated showing weakness and telling people about her problems. Her mother had instilled that trait in her, too. She sighed. If she was going to tell someone, it might as well be here and now. The safety of Albert's room was a good setting for late-night confessions.

The room was dark but for a night-light in the shape of a star. She was tired but comfortable in her snug chair, and the only noise she had for company was the quiet breathing of a sleeping baby.

Of course, it helped that her conversation partner was over a thousand miles away and a stranger; a nice, harmless, faraway stranger. If ever there was a time to open up and admit her failures, surely this was it. She watched the reply appear on her screen.

> **BlackVelvetBitches:** Huh. So, the creative muse (or whatever) isn't helping you out?

Isabella sighed again as she typed.

> **IsabellaMartinez1:** I suppose not. It's very strange. When I was working full time, I seemed to be teeming with ideas, but now that I can write—well, they all seem subpar or done to death. Nothing I write is good enough.

There was a pause before BlackVelvetBitches' reply came in. Isabella wondered if the trainer had gotten distracted, or if she was pondering what to say. Maybe this confession had been a bad idea.

> **BlackVelvetBitches:** Good enough for who? You? Or for the readers? Or for some publisher?

Isabella frowned while answering.

> **IsabellaMartinez1:** Everyone and anyone, as it stands right now. It's atrocious.

> **BlackVelvetBitches:** I'm sure it's not that bad! Isn't all writing supposed to seem predictable to the writer, because it came from your brain? I think I read that somewhere.

Isabella looked up as Alberto fidgeted a little and almost woke. But he settled once more, and Isabella went back to her iPad.

> **IsabellaMartinez1:** Oh, it's not that it's predictable. At least, I don't think so. It's more that I'm not sure if my take on it is too personal and won't be relative to others.

BlackVelvetBitches: Well, I can't help you there. If you need a good workout to clear the cobwebs and get your frustration out, I'm your woman. Writing tips...not really something I do. I mean, I could read what you've written, if you want a guinea pig, but I'm not much of a reader. Unless it's comics. If you've written about Batwoman, count me in!

Isabella realized she was smiling as she typed her reply. It seemed impossible not to smile at Erin's messages.

IsabellaMartinez1: No, I'm afraid not. It's just fairy tales rewritten for our time. Putting Little Red Riding Hood as a child star in Hollywood and Cinderella as a homeless person in New York.

BlackVelvetBitches: Oh, cool! Not my usual thing, but I'd read it.

IsabellaMartinez1: I'm glad to hear it. I think it can work if I get the feel of the stories just right. I have to constantly guard myself to make sure I don't make the tales too upsetting for the readers.

Isabella rolled her head from side to side, stretching out her neck, as she waited for Erin's reply. She needed to do something about the suffering muscles in her back and neck before they seized up completely. *Perhaps a massage would help?* She twisted right and left, feeling a line of pain shooting down between her shoulder blades. *No, that would mean leaving Alberto alone with someone else.* And it would mean undressing, at least partly, in front of a stranger. She had always hated that feeling of...being exposed. Vulnerable. Scrutinized.

BlackVelvetBitches: Okay. Aren't fairy tales supposed to be pretty, well, not upsetting?

IsabellaMartinez1: My mother told me a lot of fairy tales as a child. She never told me the watered-down and child-appropriate new versions of them, though. No Disney interpretations or books with pretty pictures. She told me folk tales and Grimm's fairy tales in all their original, bloody and cruel glory. She said that life was vicious and dangerous and that those stories would prepare me for that far better than the modern versions.

BlackVelvetBitches: Whoa! Intense mom, there!

Isabella scoffed and looked up at the ceiling. In her head, she could hear her mother's simple "you'll get over it," dripping with contempt, as she countered Isabella's complaints about having nightmares and not wanting to hear those stories anymore.

In a way, she did get over it. She grew to live with the nightmares and the dark images in her head until they became normal for her. Nevertheless, she wondered if her need to write about those fairy tales now was a way to deal with her childhood trauma, and she wondered what other damage they might have done to her.

IsabellaMartinez1: Oh, you have no idea, Miss Black. I'd like to change the topic, though.

There was a pause until Erin replied.

BlackVelvetBitches: "Miss Black," huh? I like it. No one has called me that in ages.

Alberto started fussing again, and this time he didn't settle. Isabella saw the signs and typed a quick apology and goodbye, just in case she didn't come back online.

Just as Isabella put the iPad down, Alberto started bawling his eyes out. She picked him up and rubbed his back, as she walked around the small room with him.

She decided that she wasn't going to go online later and try to find Erin again. She'd bared enough of her soul to a stranger already. It was hard for her to believe that she'd just told someone about her fears regarding her writing and disclosed—even to a tiny degree—her most closely kept secret, what Mother was like. Some things were better if not spoken of, and that was the best way to deal with Mother. Stoic silence was the way Isabella lived her life, and it wasn't going to change just because Erin Black was easy to talk to, no matter how tempting the concept was.

Isabella sat down to feed Alberto and emphatically snapped her iPad cover closed.

Chapter 5

Another Night, Another Chat

THE ABRUPT ENDING TO LAST night's chat had been disappointing. All throughout the day, but especially during her long workout in the evening, Erin had wondered if something she'd said had made Isabella leave so fast.

It was impossible for Erin not to be taken aback by how much she wanted to make their friendship stick. She wasn't used to that. Her loner existence—or maybe she should say *introvert ways*—was just what she wanted. But not only did she want to remain friends with Isabella, she wanted to become better friends with her. There was no doubt that Isabella was a witty, intelligent woman, and Erin's curiosity was certainly piqued by her.

This wasn't the norm for Erin. It wasn't even close. And she couldn't help but wonder if maybe loneliness was driving her desire to know Isabella better. After all, outside of the forced social interaction with people at work—which was the downside of her job—she didn't really talk to people these days. Not even her old friends. Sure, she was on friendly terms with Riley, but that was still a working affiliation. At least, that was the relationship Erin tried to maintain with her, despite Riley's constant forays across the professional boundaries Erin had established. Besides, they never talked about stuff that mattered. She made a mental note to tell Isabella about what had happened earlier with Riley.

Isabella was different from most of her friends, and that interested her. Plus, it was fun to chat with her. The cliché of "time flies" was certainly true when Erin spoke to Isabella, and she wanted more of that.

The laptop was on, and Skype was open. She tried to pretend that she wasn't searching out IsabellaMartinez1 in her online contacts list. It was almost midnight, after all.

Her eyes opened wide, as she found what she had been trying not to look for, Isabella's username with a green dot next to it. She was online. Erin fist-pumped the air and opened a window to talk to Isabella.

> **BlackVelvetBitches:** Hey there, Ms. Writer. How are you and the lil' stressed-out man tonight?

Happily, Isabella's reply came in right away.

> **IsabellaMartinez1:** We're fine. Alberto has just fallen asleep after a little feed, and I am researching Germanic folklore. How are you?

> **BlackVelvetBitches:** Well, neither sleeping after a good meal nor researching weird stuff. I was actually stretching after a long session at the gym.

> **IsabellaMartinez1:** You had a client this late?

Erin stretched her arms over her head and heard a faint pop from her rotator cuff as the tension let go. Then she bent forward to type again.

> **BlackVelvetBitches:** No, I was doing it for my own fitness, to work off some steam, and to digest the day a bit. Man, you wouldn't believe the crazy stuff that happened today!

> **IsabellaMartinez1:** I'm a writer, Erin. I can imagine a great deal and believe a large amount of it. Try me.

Erin smiled and began to reply.

> **BlackVelvetBitches:** Fine. You asked for it, lady. So, I have this client called Riley. Background: She trains with me once or twice a week, depending on when she's been on an all-night bender and what shape she's in the next day. She's a social butterfly and a real free spirit, and doesn't care what people think about her. Anyway, I had a session booked with her, and she showed up in a

tank top and a pair of shorts that were so tight I wasn't sure she could move in them. I didn't say anything about it, obviously.

Erin clicked *send* to make this long story readable and not just one huge block of text. Then she picked up where she left off.

BlackVelvetBitches: We started working out, and I had planned a leg day for her. About ten squats in, those tight shorts ripped! It was so loud, like in a sitcom or something. She wasn't all that embarrassed, though. She was just laughing like crazy, and then she just—get this—took them off, put 'em on the ground, and kept doing squats! I asked if she didn't want to stop or go home and get another pair of shorts, but she just said that it was fine because her underwear was Adidas, so it should count as workout clothes! Can you believe her confidence?

She clicked *send* again and took a breath. She didn't want this to come out wrong.

BlackVelvetBitches: And, yeah, the hipsters did say Adidas and weren't too skimpy, but they were still, very clearly, underwear. Besides, everyone around us had heard the shorts rip and had watched her just pull them off and keep going. Several people stopped and stared. I tried to get them all to go back to working out, but everyone seemed totally stunned. In the end, the manager of the gym came over and asked her to put shorts or pants on before carrying on. Guess what she did?

Isabella's reply appeared right away.

IsabellaMartinez1: Oh, I'm sure I couldn't guess.

BlackVelvetBitches: She said "fine." Went to her locker and got her towel, tied it around her waist, and then walked back to me and asked if we could do something which wouldn't make her drop her towel. I swear, she's my hero for being so chill. BUT it did mean trying to find moves that targeted the right muscle groups while keeping her damn towel in place. We were watched the whole time, which is something I'm not a big fan of.

Erin almost scoffed at her own understatement. She hated being stared at. It was the legacy of a child used to being surveyed and then ignored by potential adoptive parents. But Isabella didn't need to know that.

> **IsabellaMartinez1:** I can see why not. That sounds like quite the farce. Are your sessions always so eventful?

> **BlackVelvetBitches:** Yeah, it was completely ridiculous. Oh, and it didn't help that she kept telling me about her sexy date with this hot model between reps. Crazy! And no, they're not.

> **IsabellaMartinez1:** This is so interesting. Training really has its own challenges and joys, doesn't it? I've never spoken to a personal trainer before. Maybe you could tell me about your other clients today? Even the boring ones. I want to know what a day in your work life might look like.

A little embarrassed by the attention, Erin gave an in-depth description of the clients she had trained that day. Forty minutes later, she had given every detail she could remember and, according to Isabella's replies, made the other woman laugh loud enough to almost wake the baby at one point.

Happy with the way the conversation was going, Erin finished her tirade by saying that was surely enough about her day and asking what Isabella had been up to.

> **IsabellaMartinez1:** Nothing interesting.

> **BlackVelvetBitches:** Oh, come on. Something must have happened? Something about Alberto or about your writing? How is the fairy tale book coming along?

> **IsabellaMartinez1:** Hmm. Fine. Alberto has a rash on his neck, and I had to go out and get a cream for that, but I'm sure you don't want to hear about it. I've gotten some writing done today but not as much as I'd like. I did, however, clean my little writing nook downstairs.

> **BlackVelvetBitches:** You've got a writing nook?

IsabellaMartinez1: It's my favorite part of the house. The desk is nothing special in itself, but it has the antique pen set that my father bought me when I left my job to write, and a gorgeous desk lamp I brought home from a trip to Tangier ten years ago. Oh, and a bookshelf for all my resource material and a few of my favorite novels.

Erin was impressed to be talking to someone who had been to Tangier, mainly because her most exotic trip had been to Las Vegas. Although, she wasn't sure where exactly Tangier was and hurried to google it before replying.

BlackVelvetBitches: Your little writing corner sounds really pretty and cozy. You'll have to take a picture of it and send it to me.

This time the reply took a while to come in. Erin wondered if Alberto had woken up or if Isabella was pondering whether or not she wanted to send Erin photos of her home.

IsabellaMartinez1: I can do better than that. I am going to go down and make a cup of coffee. If you like, I could bring the iPad and make a video call to you when we're downstairs? Me and Alberto sometimes have video calls with my parents. That's why I got Skype in the first place. It would be an easier way for you to see my desk and bookshelf. It would just be one-way video, obviously, so I won't see you.

BlackVelvetBitches: Yeah, sounds great! Are you bringing Alberto?

Erin couldn't help feeling excited to see some of this stranger's home. She wasn't usually this curious, but now she couldn't wait to nose around a little. She had a feeling that she was about to see glimpses of a fancy house that cost as much to heat per day as her own monthly rent.

IsabellaMartinez1: No, I can't film and carry him.

Erin's brows knitted, both at the curtness of the reply and the contents of it.

BlackVelvetBitches: But what if he wakes up? I thought you always brought him with you in case he wakes his dad up with the crying?

There was a long pause before Isabella replied.

IsabellaMartinez1: Well then, I suppose Richard will just have to wake up. I'm sure he will fall back asleep again soon enough.

Erin raised her eyebrows at this change of outlook.

BlackVelvetBitches: Cool. Go get your coffee, and show me where the writing magic happens!

IsabellaMartinez1: All right. I'll go downstairs and then call you. Hang on a moment.

Erin watched the screen intently, as she took a few sips of her coffee. After a short while, a request to answer a video call from IsabellaMartinez1 came in, and Erin clicked the button to accept.

Her laptop screen filled with the image of a dimly lit space. Isabella was clearly holding the iPad like a camera and filming the room. She walked toward a corner desk and bookshelf, showing Erin the writing area she had described.

Squinting, Erin saw that one of the bigger books on the shelf was titled *The Art of Writing* in a large, clear font. The others she couldn't make out. She saw the antique pen set and the desk lamp from Tangier that Isabella had told her about.

Then a quiet voice spoke. It sounded deep and sultry, but serious, and as smooth as melted chocolate.

"Can you see? Is it too dark in here? The light is on in the hall, but I can turn on the one in here as well, if you'd like?"

Erin found herself shaking her head before she realized that Isabella couldn't see her. She cleared her throat and answered in a croak, which was as much due to being silent for hours as to being blown away by what she was seeing.

"No, it's fine. It looks really nice and cozy. You seem to have a lovely home."

Immediately, she wondered if she sounded like some 1950s housewife visiting her neighbor. *"Lovely home?" What the hell, Black?*

"Thank you. I did a lot of decorating when I was pregnant and too restless to sit still and write. There isn't a detail in this house I didn't plan out meticulously. Anyway, I should make the coffee and go back upstairs before Alberto wakes up."

Suddenly, instead of showing the room, the iPad's camera was focused on Isabella's face, and Erin could see a brunette who was frowning as she quietly muttered, "Can I hang up without losing the chat?"

She saw Isabella's hand move around the camera and guessed that she was pushing different parts of the screen. She wondered if Isabella had tried to turn the camera off and instead reversed it to film her face, but that thought vanished from her mind as quickly as it had arrived. Erin knew she should answer Isabella's question. But she couldn't. In fact, she couldn't even remember what the question had been. Her brain was too fried by what she was seeing.

The woman on the screen was drop-dead gorgeous. She wasn't wearing any makeup, but her eyelashes were long and dark and framed a pair of brown eyes that changed from espresso colored to latte as they caught the light from the hallway. Isabella's jaw, cheeks, and nose were all unusually symmetrical, like a classic movie star. There seemed to be a little cut above her top lip. Those lips looked as soft as silk. In fact, all of Isabella's olive skin looked incredibly soft.

Erin tore her gaze away from the features, but only long enough to see more of Isabella. Cascades of sable-colored hair fell to her shoulders, and below, Erin could see a collar of what looked like gray pajamas.

She was staring openmouthed, and Erin closed her jaw so quickly that there was a loud click of her teeth. Luckily, Isabella was too preoccupied with her technical difficulties to notice.

"I think I've found it. I'll hit this button, and I should hang up without closing down our chat window. I'll go make coffee, and I'll talk to you when I get back upstairs," Isabella said.

"Um, you don't have to close it down quite yet. I mean, unless you want to."

With a frown, Erin bit her lower lip. How could she be this pathetic? This was a stranger who was probably straight and certainly in a relationship, and here she was, jumping through hoops to keep the camera focused on that beautiful face just a little longer. She cursed herself for being so ridiculous.

"Oh. All right. I can show you the kitchen, I suppose," Isabella replied politely.

Erin could tell from the motion of the camera and the sounds of quiet steps that Isabella was walking to the kitchen. The camera angle was still reversed, and in the light from the hall, Erin watched her features.

She couldn't help but squint and have another look at Isabella's lips. The little outline above her upper lip was a scar, not a cut. Without thinking, Erin spoke out loud.

"How did you get that scar?"

The camera stopped, and Isabella looked down at the iPad with a look of horror.

"You can see me? I thought the camera was on the other side?"

Erin froze. Her lost thought about Isabella not knowing she had reversed the camera was indeed right, and she hadn't spoken up about it until now. *Shit!*

"You mean you didn't know the camera had reversed? Um, I think you turned the camera around to yourself as you were trying to figure out how to hang up without ending the chat. I did wonder about that, but I forgot to ask you. I'm so sorry, Isabella."

Instinctively, Isabella's hand flew up to smooth down her hair. She was frowning fiercely.

"I see. How do I turn it back? I wasn't really ready to be on camera tonight. I must look dreadful."

Erin's mouth decided to, once more, exclude her brain from her reply and blurted out the first thing that came to mind.

"You kidding me? You look like a freakin' goddess!"

The woman on the screen rolled her eyes but couldn't quite hide a smile.

"That's very kind of you to say, but it's obviously a white lie. I'm a breastfeeding mom in my pajamas, without makeup, who hasn't slept properly for weeks. The bags under my eyes probably have bags of their own."

The dark shadows had been obvious, but those eyes were so beautiful. They'd drawn her gaze away from pretty much everything else.

"If I looked half as good as you when fully prettied up, I'd be ecstatic. Stop complaining, and go show me that coffee."

Isabella relaxed visibly.

"Fine. But first tell me how to turn the camera."

While Erin explained, Isabella followed the directions until the camera no longer showed her face but the floor at her slipper-clad feet.

Erin forced herself not to sigh with disappointment, then she scolded herself for objectifying her new friend. She remembered what her ex, Katie, had used to say, "Straight girls are friends, not food." It might be a bit crude, but the message was clear, and it was one Erin needed to keep in mind now.

Erin fought down any thoughts about how attractive Isabella was and just focused on getting to know her. She started with observing the kitchen that Isabella wanted to show her. The floor in the kitchen looked like marbled tiles—pretty but cold. She understood why Isabella was wearing slippers.

After a second or two, she heard Isabella whisper a walking commentary.

"So this is the kitchen. As you can see, I went with dove-gray units with fully integrated appliances and white and gray floor tiles to match."

Damn that voice was lovely. Erin could listen to just about anything spoken with that satisfyingly warm and deep sound. Erin closed her eyes and listened with a happy smirk. Then she snapped herself out of it. This was not being *friendly*.

Isabella was still talking. In her reverie, Erin had missed some of the details about the kitchen. Hopefully, nothing too important.

"And this cabinet here is where the coffee resides." Isabella said, while using her free hand to open a cabinet that showed neat rows of dry foodstuffs.

She picked up a bright-red foil package with black lettering that was difficult to read, especially in the semi-lit kitchen. Erin could just about make out the words *Azúcar Negra* in a slanting font.

"Never seen that before," Erin said.

She was whispering too, nervous that her voice would echo in Isabella's stylishly minimalistic kitchen.

"Well, as I said, it's worth every dime. Pure coffee heaven and fair trade too."

"Awesome. How do you take it?" Erin asked.

"I believe all good coffee should be drunk black. In my opinion, milk and sugar is only for horrible coffee that needs to be diluted."

Isabella put the bag of coffee grounds on the counter and struggled with the iPad.

"I'm going to place this on its stand on the counter while I make the coffee. You can enjoy the view of the kitchen. Considering the money we spent on it, I am happy that more people get to see it."

Erin looked around to see as much as the camera angle allowed.

"Don't have many guests, huh?"

"Not a huge number, no. I tend to prefer the company of a few close friends, and Richard's friends seem to have stopped flocking to the house. Probably because I kept telling them off for dirtying up the place. They're all outdoorsy, like he is," Isabella replied with a certain tension in her voice.

Erin guessed that she had hit a sore spot and retreated back into safer territory.

"Does Richard drink this luxury coffee too?"

"No, he doesn't like the taste of coffee. He says people are crazy to drink something so bitter. He prefers herbal tea. Lemon and ginger seems to be what he favors these days."

Erin frowned. "No caffeine? Dude's hardcore. How does anyone adult without caffeine? If you can't have it for medical reasons, fine, but by choice—whoa. I mean, even my health-nut colleagues drink green tea, which has some caffeine in it."

Erin wondered if she was supposed to have heard Isabella's sigh.

"He says that his job is invigorating enough for him, and he doesn't need what he calls 'a crutch.'"

Erin couldn't hide a derisive scoff. Then she froze. She was in the rudeness danger zone now. She relaxed when she heard Isabella give a little chuckle and say, "Yes, exactly."

Something warm buzzed in the pit of Erin's stomach. That little laugh, it sounded so damn attractive and musical. It was like the notes bypassed Erin's ears and went straight to her belly.

Isabella was a woman who didn't appear to laugh a whole lot, and Erin had just made her chuckle. She almost felt a bit of a high. That aside, she wished she didn't sense the sadness that emanated from Isabella.

Erin rubbed her furrowed forehead. She wanted to ask about the relationship between Isabella and Richard. So far it didn't sound very happy or very romantic. But even she wasn't socially clumsy enough to just come out and ask what was going on there.

The sounds of coffee being brewed stopped, and the quiet spluttering of the coffee pot took over. Erin desperately thought of what to say while she chewed the inside of her cheek.

All her ideas stopped dead, when Isabella stepped in the way of the camera. She was clearly moving to get what Erin assumed was a cup out of the cupboard. She saw a full-body view of Isabella. She had been right about the gray pajamas. They looked shiny, maybe silk.

Isabella moved quietly, elegantly, and Erin couldn't stop her eyes from taking in the contours of soft curves and the thin waist the fitted pajamas hinted at.

Dammit, you're objectifying again. Bad lesbian, she cursed inwardly and looked away.

When she glanced back, Isabella was gone again and talking about her caffeine intake.

"I gave up coffee the first months of carrying Alberto. Abstinence turned me into more of a monster than I thought possible. When I shouted at my very sweet and mild-mannered father, I gave up and allowed myself one cup a day. This size of cup."

Isabella held out a small coffee cup in front of the iPad.

"That looks barely big enough to hold an espresso." Erin was appalled.

Isabella hummed her agreement, and Erin had to hold on to the seat of her chair to keep herself from thinking about the lovely low purr in that hum.

"When Alberto was born, and he never slept through the night because of his troublesome tummy, I asked my doctor if it was advisable to up the dosage to two cups a day. He said that it would be the equivalent of a normal mug of coffee per day and that he thought it was fine. So here I am. Having my second cup."

"Makes sense to me. You gotta keep yourself sane to be able to look after him. If coffee allows that, then go for it. It's not like our moms didn't drink coffee or tea when we were babies, right?"

"I believe Mother even smoked at the start of her pregnancy. Probably explains a lot about me," Isabella quipped dryly.

"Yeah, that explains why you walk around looking perfect when you should be a mess, I suppose. There's something really weird about that, for sure," Erin said.

She tensed. Was that acceptable as platonic friends, or did she just sound like she was hitting on Isabella?

Isabella gave another of those soft chuckles. "You're very kind. I should pay you to give me a compliment like that every day."

"Send me some of that pricey coffee, and you'll have paid for a nightly compliment for, like, two years."

Another chuckle, and then Erin heard the sound of pouring. Isabella must have moved to the side to get to her cup, because suddenly Erin could see her hip on her screen. As she turned ever so slightly, Erin saw the profile of a very nicely rounded behind.

The thoughts running through Erin's head were definitely not platonic. She hated herself for not being able to stop them. She clenched her jaw shut, painfully tight.

"Um, Isabella. I'm gonna go and try for some sleep, actually. I doubt it will work, but since muscles heal during sleep, it might be the only way to make sure I don't wake up tense after that hardcore gym session earlier. Sorry to abandon you right when you got your coffee and all, but you know…"

Isabella sounded confused as she said, "all right," but then collected and poised again as she followed up with, "If you think you can get some sleep, then you should obviously try. I'm sure Alberto will wake up any moment now, anyway. And I should be getting on with some writing."

"Okay, cool," Erin replied, eager to end the call.

"I suppose I'll see you in a normal text chat tomorrow night or perhaps the night after. Take care, and I do hope you get some sleep."

Erin didn't comment on how unlikely her sleeping was, she just tried to sound normal as she replied, "Yeah, sure. I hope lil' guy lets you have a few hours, too. Talk later. Bye."

She hung up. With a sigh, she ran a hand over her face. That had turned into a disaster. She had pretty much drooled over every part of this poor woman and then run away in the middle of what promised to be a really interesting chat.

The worst part was that she wondered if she would have been almost as bad if she hadn't seen and heard Isabella but just text chatted. She just seemed to be geared toward liking this woman, liking her a little too much. Was it just her recent loneliness and celibate lifestyle confusing her? Somehow, she didn't think it was that simple.

There was no way she was going to sleep or be able to focus on anything meaningful, so Erin threw herself on the bed, which doubled as couch in her small apartment, and turned on the TV. She found an old rerun of a sitcom to watch.

A whole two seconds passed, before she started thinking about Isabella. Had she upset her by just leaving like that? It didn't seem likely, but then Isabella was that cool, classy kind of person who, in Erin's experience, tended to have a good poker face. Erin couldn't even start to guess what she was thinking. She tried to focus on the sitcom and getting sleepy.

After a while, she gave up and rolled over to open her bedside table drawer. She fished out an old pill dispenser and shook one of the turquoise capsules into the palm of her hand. She hated how sleeping pills made her feel the day after, but she wasn't going to stop obsessing unless she could knock her brain out. This was a better option than five shots of bourbon.

She went into the bathroom, poured some water into her hand, and swallowed the capsule. Then she brushed her teeth and went back to the bed. After about an hour of trying to focus on watching TV, she was lost in fevered dreams, chasing something she needed without knowing what it was.

Chapter 6

The Past Is Always with Us

THE NEXT MORNING, ISABELLA WENT down to breakfast and yelped when she walked straight into Richard. The collision was painless, merely startling. They ended up looking at each other in mutual confusion.

"G-good morning," he mumbled, voice gruff with sleep.

"Richard. I thought you'd be on your way to work by now?"

"I got the chance to sleep in. I'm going in a little late today because I have a meeting that'll drag on later. Erm, you shouldn't expect me home for dinner. Sorry, didn't I tell you about that?"

For a moment, Isabella wasn't sure. Could she have forgotten? With a sense of sadness, she realized that they hadn't had any meaningful conversations in a very long time.

"I don't think so. We…we haven't spoken much lately."

He scratched at his unshaven chin. "No, I guess we haven't. Sorry. I should have made a point to mention it. I hope you didn't have big dinner plans."

"Nothing special, no. I'll just make dinner for us both and put yours in a Tupperware box in the fridge for you. You can heat it up later, if you want it."

He smiled, looking a little sheepish. "Yeah. And if me and the guys grab takeaway tonight, I can have it for lunch tomorrow."

"Yes. Good idea."

"Right. Thanks for doing that."

"Of course," Isabella answered.

They were silent for a moment. It felt so awkward and so fragile. Isabella wracked her brain for something to say.

"Alberto actually got some sleep last night."

Richard put his hands in his pockets and seemed to be trying to look relaxed. It wasn't working. "Oh, did he? That's good."

"Yes."

"Did you?" Richard asked.

"Pardon?"

"Did you get some sleep," Richard clarified.

Isabella groaned at her own stupidity. "Right, sorry. Not quite awake yet. Yes, I slept a little. You?"

"Slept like the dead."

"That's good," Isabella said.

Was the clock in the kitchen ticking louder than usual?

Richard cleared his throat. "Yes. Um. So, where's Alberto now?"

"Upstairs. Sleeping. I just changed and fed him, and then he fell right back to asleep."

"I see. Well, we should probably get ourselves fed too," he said.

Isabella nodded, grateful that the stilted conversation seemed to be over.

She went for the cabinet where her coffee was kept and opened the door just as Richard reached for the cabinet next to her. They almost bumped into each other again. Instead they both stepped back quickly—Richard seemed as eager to avoid contact with her as she was with him.

"Oh, sorry. I was just going to get my granola," he explained.

"That's quite all right. Go ahead."

Isabella moved back another step and watched Richard gingerly reach past her to get to his granola. Were they really so terrified of touching each other? Why? They were lovers once. They were partners in this family. Now they edged around each other like strangers afraid of bothering each other in any way. When had this happened? Why hadn't she noticed it happening? She gave a long exhale. That was part of the problem, wasn't it? She had noticed. She'd just never bothered to question it before.

He stopped mid-move. "You know what? I think I'll stop somewhere for breakfast before going to work. That way I won't be in your way."

Isabella suddenly felt even worse. "Oh, don't leave on my account. This is your house too. I can wait until you're done."

He smiled and shook his head. "It's easier if I get something to eat on the way. It can be a treat to celebrate getting the morning off."

"If you think it's best," she said hesitantly.

"I do. I'll just go up and quickly shave and get dressed. Then I'll be out of your hair."

"Why don't you stop in to kiss Alberto goodbye on the way? You rarely get to see him in the morning."

Richard shrugged, seeming distracted by his watch. "I wouldn't want to wake him. Let him sleep. I'm sure I'll see him tonight."

"Oh. Okay, if you're sure."

She could hear the confusion in her own voice and hoped it hadn't sounded judgmental. They both knew he could give Alberto a quick kiss on the head without waking him. Clearly, Richard either didn't see the need or didn't have the desire to do so. She wasn't sure which option upset her most, the ignorance of his son's needs or indifference to them. *Be fair, Isabella. He's a good man, and a good father. Perhaps he's just uncomfortable with such a small baby. It's not uncommon among men for that to be the case. Look at all the time he spends with Joshua.* The five-year-old son of Richard's prior marriage certainly benefitted from the huge amount of time Richard devoted to him on the weekends, and it was clear to see how much he loved the boy.

She watched him walk out the door and wondered what it would take for him to be as comfortable with Alberto as he was with Joshua. A niggling voice at the back of her head was quick to answer. *You giving him a chance, perhaps? Instead of hovering over the child like the overprotective lioness all the time. He's Alberto's father. He won't hurt him if you leave them alone together for an hour.*

She heard him walk upstairs, as she got her Azúcar Negra out and began to brew the life-giving coffee before serving herself some yogurt, topped with nuts and honey. As she ate, Richard came back downstairs.

As he was lacing up his boots, he said, "I'm going to head out then. Have a good day, Isabella."

She quickly swallowed her mouthful. "Goodbye. You have a good day, as well. I'll see you tonight."

Richard picked up his keys and jacket. He looked at her as if he was thinking about something. He took a step in her direction. Then he backed away again.

Turning to the door, he waved at her and left.

She stared after him.

A wave? Since when do we wave to each other? We used to at least kiss each other on the cheek. Should I have kissed him on the cheek? She tried to remember the last time he had kissed her when he left for work. She couldn't.

Worse than that, she realized she didn't care. Worse still, she was relieved. Relieved that she hadn't had to pretend to be receptive. The kiss would just have been unpleasant, and stilted, and…fake.

Besides, her coffee was ready.

Isabella had other things on her mind, things that were just as difficult, yet at the same time easier for her to focus on. She couldn't shake her conversation with Erin the night before. Talking about her relationship with her mother brought up thoughts she usually buried deep.

As she put her little cup of coffee on the table, she heard Alberto make mewling noises from upstairs, and went to fetch him. He soon fell back asleep once he was with her in the kitchen, and she finished the last of her yogurt.

The house was silent again. Isabella sat at the table, sipping her coffee, a feeling of discomfort lodged deep in her stomach.

She picked up her phone and flicked through her text messages, quickly finding the one she was looking for. Her sister, Marie, casually informing Isabella that she'd stopped dating her latest love interest. The very successful and equally dull Steve.

That sort of text didn't require a reply, and Isabella had to admit that she'd decided not to, just to ward off a conversation. She loved Marie, she truly did. Yet she avoided talking to her for long periods of time. They were too different and that really showed when they spoke for too long.

After last night's conversation with Erin, the appeal of connecting with someone who knew what it was like growing up with Judith Martinez was undeniable. Even though Marie had been taken in by their family as a teenager and only had to put up with Judith for a few years before she moved out. Besides, it would be a good distraction from thinking about her encounter with Richard. She decided to reply and wondered about what to say.

Sorry to hear that. To use a vile but correct cliché, there's plenty more fish in the sea. You'll find the right man for you soon.

Considerably less acerbic and more sisterly than her normal replies, but she was satisfied she'd reached out and done her bit. She knew there might be a text back but felt her reply had been phrased in such a way that it wasn't inviting a long conversation. Instead the phone rang. *Damn.* Isabella reluctantly tapped the screen to answer.

Before she even had time to say hello, she heard the words, "A magnificently good morning to you, darling sister!"

Isabella groaned. "What was it about that message that made you feel the need to call me, Marie?"

"Ooooh, charming as ever. Maybe I missed you? Thanks for replying, by the way. Even if you didn't need to. Does that mean you missed me too?"

Isabella smiled as she shook her head at her impossible, cutesy, chirpy, infuriating sibling. "It meant that I have a sisterly duty to make sure you're all right. Steve's not in the picture anymore, and while I know you weren't that invested in him, I thought I should check on you anyway." It wasn't a complete lie. She had planned to check up on Marie soon.

"Aw, thank you. You know me. I bounce back in two seconds flat. He was too settled in negative thought patterns for me, and I was relieved when he called it quits. Still, you know how I hate being single. I know I'm supposed to use this time to draw strength from being untethered and center myself. But I really miss the partnership and physical affection."

Isabella merely hummed in response and walked over to Alberto who was writhing a bit, clearly having some stomach issues.

"Another year without marriage and procreation for me. Not exactly the progress a member of the Martinez family is expected to be making, huh?" Marie said, her cheerful tone faltering a little.

Just like that, they were talking about their mother. Isabella felt herself freeze up. Deep down, wasn't that what she'd wanted but been unable to admit? To talk to someone who understood? Someone who remembered?

"Have you told her and Daddy that you broke up with Steve?"

Marie laughed mirthlessly, something rare for the happy-go-lucky woman. "I sure have."

Isabella fiddled with the hem of Alberto's trouser leg, before she caught herself and stilled her hands. "And?"

"And…well, you know how she has certain expectations, and she'll do anything to steer you toward them? And how she can talk to you until you get things all muddled and feel that her choices for you are more important than your own?"

"Oh, absolutely," Isabella replied.

"Well, she nearly convinced me that I should try to get him back. She talked for ages about how it was more important that he was financially stable and came from a good family, than it was to enjoy his company. I honestly wonder what world she lives in sometimes."

"One where she knows better than everyone else and there is a strict social hierarchy to obey," Isabella replied, feeling herself grimace as she said the words.

"Yes. I suppose so. Still, she means well. I think. I don't mean to excuse her behavior, of course. I know she's a lot harder on you than she is on me." Marie paused. "You know, that's actually a bit of a mystery. I mean, you've got the man and the child, so you're settled and giving her grandchildren as per the Martinez expectation. You were wildly successful in your career. However, it still isn't enough. She's still not happy." She hummed. "Maybe it's because you're her biological daughter and I'm not. That makes sense, right? I get more of a break because I'm a Bowman and not a Martinez."

Isabella let out a breath. "Maybe. Which is ridiculous, as you are just as much a part of this family as I am. Let me set you straight, though. I get no points for having a man in my life for two reasons. One, we're not married, and two, he doesn't pass for what Mother thinks is "acceptable." Richard doesn't have the kind of job Mother thinks is fitting for a man of standing, he doesn't come from a noble background, nor is he a social climber. As far as she's concerned, he's one step above a vagrant. Barely. You know that. I've sat through enough dinners with her complaining about your relationships to be under no illusion that she doesn't do the same to you. I'm sure you've heard all that and more, straight from the horse's mouth, as they say."

"Mm, true, she said as much to me again when I last spoke to her a couple of days ago. I think she was trying to pry information out of me."

Isabella felt her stomach knot. It was an irrational, emotional response. She was a grown woman, in charge of her own life, yet still her mother had this power over her. This ability to affect her on such a visceral level that she felt physical discomfort, sometimes even pain, at the thought of Judith's intervention, or rather meddling, in her life. "What about?"

Marie hummed again, sounding reluctant to be the bearer of bad news. "Whether the two of you are getting married soon. I gathered from her tone that she thinks you should be married at your age, but she's still sort of happy you're not, because it's Richard."

"God, she has to know everything. This is just like when she used to read my diaries and my letters."

"I know. But she does love you. I believe that with all my heart."

Isabella scoffed. "You also believe that if you've been chronically ill you can get better through positive thinking alone."

"You *can*. It's been scientifically proven," Marie replied in a singsong voice.

Isabella hummed noncommittally, not ready to start up this debate again. Last time, she had ended up telling Marie she was "as brainless as a turnip" and didn't want a repeat. She didn't like herself when she was insulting her sister.

A gurgle drew her attention. Alberto's writhing was increasing, and his face was turning pink.

"Marie, I'm going to have to go. Alberto is having a bad day with his stomach."

"Aww. Of course. Kiss little Beto from me. Talk soon?"

"Yes. We'll talk soon, *hermanita*," Isabella said and disconnected to quickly pick up Alberto.

Later that night, Isabella walked back upstairs with her cup of coffee. Halfway up, she heard Alberto crying. She hurried but couldn't rush too much or she'd spill her black coffee on the cream-colored carpet.

When she finally reached the door to Alberto's nursery, Richard came out of their shared bedroom. A title it didn't live up to, as Isabella only slept there during daytime naps with Alberto when he was particularly fussy and wouldn't sleep without her next to him.

Richard rubbed his face drowsily. "Is everything okay?"

"Yes, everything's fine. I just went down and get some coffee. Apparc. he woke up and felt all alone." She sighed inwardly. *Something he and I hav. in common.*

She hurried through the door, put her coffee down, and picked up the wailing Alberto. He quieted a bit, as she rubbed slow, gentle circles on his back.

She laid him on the seat of the armchair, so she could rub little circles on his belly as the doctor had showed them at Alberto's last checkup. The motion had its usual good result, and the mewling baby let out a burp.

Alberto's little face relaxed, as he went from loud whining to hesitant cooing. The tension drained from his body, and soon he began to happily kick his little feet up at her where she was hunched over him. She dodged the kicks with practiced ease and smiled at her little prince.

"That's much better isn't it, *mi corazón?*"

He cooed in response and kicked a little higher. Isabella grabbed his onesie-clad foot and kissed it. She'd all but forgotten Richard's presence, assuming he would have returned to bed as soon as he knew that everything was all right, until he spoke next to her.

"That little belly of yours isn't very nice, huh, pal?"

He crouched next to Isabella and softly patted Alberto's stomach with his big hand.

Isabella watched him from the corner of her eye. Richard could be such a great father to Alberto. He was warm, kind, and playful. All the traits he showed when he was with his other son, Joshua.

Richard wasn't as close to Alberto, and she worried again that she was the reason. She knew very well that she prevented people from making a connection with Alberto by keeping him to herself, even when it came to Richard. She just couldn't seem to stop herself.

Alberto was her everything. He was the child she thought she could never have, and he had taught her about the person she wanted to be. Gone was the ruthless, workaholic, Isabella Martinez. In her place was a woman who was happy spending hours bathing, putting on lotion, and cuddling a little baby.

"Do you need a break? Want me to rock him to sleep?" Richard asked while barely masking a yawn.

it. I'm up anyway and need to drink my coffee. You go

e said, with what sounded like relief to her.

to kiss Alberto's tummy, then straightened up to kiss
Had she blinked, she would have missed it. It was the
quickest brush of the lips she'd ever experienced and the chaste kiss left her
indifferent.

Sometimes, she looked at him and wondered who he was, this man who
worked so diligently, who spent his weekends hiking and going on trips
through the swamplands with Joshua, and who always seemed so content.
So calm. So unfazed by the fact that he spent so little time with Alberto and
that his girlfriend refused to share his bed.

Why didn't he care? Why wasn't he upset? He was always so fair and
gallant, letting her decide what was right without discussion or dispute.
Perhaps that should be nice, she thought. But it wasn't. It was unsettling.
And for the millionth time, Isabella wondered if she and Richard had made
the right decision. It had seemed so obvious at the time.

She walked around with Alberto in her arms now, humming a lullaby
slightly out of tune. He didn't mind what her crooning sounded like, it
always calmed him. He became heavy in her arms, and she realized he was
sleeping again. She brought him back to his crib and gently tucked him in.

She sat down in her armchair and decided to write down an explanation—
or maybe it was more of an exploration—about her and Richard and how
they ended up in this relationship and in this big, quiet house. Supposedly
together, but decidedly not. She wanted—no, she needed—to make it clear
for herself how they had gotten to this point.

It had all happened so fast and it had seemed like the right thing to
do. At the time, anyway. Now, she couldn't help but wonder. She realized
she had, in fact, been wondering about it for a long time, she just hadn't
allowed herself to look too closely at the problem. Admitting there was an
issue would mean she would have to take action. That was who she was.
And she didn't see a point in acting on it. After all, was there really a better
option?

And would you deserve it if there was?

It was all so overwhelming and messy. She needed to see the chain of
events in front of her, needed to get the facts clear, and evaluate the story

like she would a piece of fiction. Maybe then she could see where they'd gone so wrong.

She opened up the writing app on her iPad and started typing quickly. The words pouring from her fingertips with an ease that her writing had lacked of late. She wrote about it all. The hardworking, no-nonsense CEO for a catering company, and the kind, gentle man she'd met in a bar, on a business trip to Florida.

He'd been there with colleagues. When one of his coworkers started hitting on Isabella, way too aggressively, he'd stepped in and put an end to the harassment. He'd been gentlemanly. Sweet. There had been no hidden motives, no plan to "screw the ice queen" like so many of the guys Isabella met back home. He'd just been harmless. He'd just been Richard. And it had been a breath of fresh air.

He was safe. She'd felt safe with him, and that was something that had been lacking in Isabella's life for as long as she could remember. Only her father had occasionally provided safety for her. And even then it had been a fleeting sense rather than the lingering one she desperately craved. When she met Richard, he'd seemed to fill that role, that need she had.

She wrote about how they went to her hotel room that night and ended up in bed. He made love to her so sweetly, listened to every word so intently, that she ignored the fact that they had nothing in common.

The next day, after singing her praises and talking about how he had never met anyone so impressive and enigmatic, he told her he was in the middle of getting a divorce from his wife but that it wasn't quite finalized. He talked about his son and how much he missed him. How he was sure that Isabella would adore him if they met. He'd seemed heartbroken. He'd seemed to need her. No one had ever needed her like he did then. And she'd never known how much she needed to be needed.

So, she'd prolonged her trip and Richard had stayed with her.

The days moved on, and soon she had to go back home to Philadelphia. She went back to work but missed those feelings of being safe, of being needed, and of being someone new. Someone other than the ice queen or the hard-assed boss at work. With Richard she could be someone loving and relaxed and not the irascible business woman, constantly on edge.

So, she kept in touch with him. Lighthearted e-mails and flirty texts, the occasional promise that they'd meet up again soon.

Eight weeks later, she found out she was pregnant. To say it was a shock would be an understatement of gargantuan proportions. She'd been told by doctors years ago that she could never have children. That she was infertile after several operations to remove ovarian cysts had left too much scarring. She even went so far as to ask the doctor to double-check, since she'd been so sure she couldn't get pregnant. But, yes, there was a little baby in there. "No doubt about it," the doctor told her with a good-natured chuckle. One she could only meet with a confused stare.

She called Richard right away. She told him she would probably get an abortion.

He was devastated, but being his usual, sweet self he told her she should do what she felt was right. That he would support her. But the disappointment that dripped from his voice like syrup left Isabella feeling so guilty she couldn't breathe.

She began thinking about being a mother. A part of her had been gravely disappointed when she'd learned she couldn't have children. A part of her she'd grieved for and thought she'd laid to rest. She had moved on, finding other goals and purposes for her life and been happy with that. Finding out that she was pregnant was beyond scary. As was the thought of discovering what kind of mother she would be. Would she turn out to be like her own mother? That fear alone was almost enough to convince her to go through with the abortion.

But a deeper part of her feared the loss of this opportunity, probably her only opportunity to have a child of her own. Uncharacteristically at a loss as to which way to turn, she confided in her father. He was thrilled and completely unable to hide it. He pointed out that this was a once-in-a-lifetime chance, since she was not supposed to be able to have children.

He told her stories about rocking her to sleep when she was a newborn, about when she thought the funniest thing in the world was her father making the rubber ducky disappear under the water in her baby bath. He also mentioned that it was a great time to start working on that book she'd always dreamt about writing. Emotional manipulation? Maybe. But she couldn't be angry with him. She knew his heart was in the right place.

Between him and Richard, she had allowed herself to be convinced. For which she was eternally grateful. Alberto was her sun and her stars, and she loved him more than she had ever known she could.

But she'd also made the decision that Alberto should have his father in his life. And a nice, stable home. Far, far away from his grandmother.

She wouldn't let her fear of becoming her mother turn her into the woman. Her son would not grow up like she had. No one would shout at Alberto or punish him unduly, like Mother had done to her. They were all going to be happy and safe in Richard's Florida sunshine.

She had talked herself into this relationship, accepting mild affection as a viable form of love. She realized that now. While Richard…well, he'd immediately jumped at the chance to start another family and had started looking for a house before Isabella had even quit her job. Whether he truly wanted a fresh start or was simply determined not to have another son grow up without him a part of his daily life, she didn't know. Maybe Richard didn't either. Whatever his reason was, she was growing more and more certain that it wasn't because he was madly in love with her.

Did he ever fall in love with me? Or was it just attraction that grew into some form of duty? His moral obligation for getting me pregnant.

She doubted she'd ever know the answer. How do you ask someone a question like that? Just how frank and deep would that conversation have to be? This was all so far out of her comfort zone.

She focused back on the chain of events. They'd moved in together on the outskirts of the Floridian town of Naples, so Richard could be close to the Everglades where much of his work took place. He spent the duration of her pregnancy looking after her. He reduced his hours, just so he could be there if she needed something. It was then she'd started to realize just how ill-suited they were.

Her fingers stiffened. As if they didn't want to type the rest. They wanted her to stop and spare her the humiliation of seeing the mess she had made of her life. She flexed, bringing life back into them before forcing them back to the iPad and on with their duty.

Where was I? Oh yes, being ill-suited.

Richard didn't understand her restlessness or her need for space. He took every hormone-driven mood swing personally, sulking for days instead of communicating. He never understood when she was being sarcastic or serious, and would take a joke to heart and ignore something heartfelt, further antagonizing Isabella. Then she'd snipe at him and they'd both be miserable. Richard, because he didn't understand what he had done wrong, and Isabella, because she felt like a cruel, miserable old bat.

They had very little to talk about, and soon she grew tired of his slow and gentle lovemaking. One night, she braved talking to him about it, despite being raised to never speak of sex, and despite the relationship being woefully low on communication. She'd asked him if they could try something different. He'd shrugged and said that he didn't see why they should as their love life was perfect. Then he fell asleep. That was the last time she attempted to fix their sexual relationship. And the last time they'd had sex.

Now, they were like brother and sister. No, more like coworkers running a company called Raise Alberto Safely.

Isabella wrote about her fear of spending the rest of her life with Richard and about how she worried she would one day snap and just scream at him, scream like Alberto would on nights when his stomach was worse than usual.

She ended the long note by writing about the question that shamed her. When would it be best to end the relationship—when Alberto was too young to miss Richard or when he had gotten a childhood with his father and grown old enough to understand why relationships didn't work out?

When she put the iPad down in her lap, she realized she had been writing the note as if she was telling the story to Erin Black. She frowned and switched off the tablet.

Obviously, she wouldn't send it to that alluring stranger in New York.

Chapter 7

The Physical Stuff

ERIN WAS IN THE GYM, hitting a punching bag but not putting much effort into it. She was just keeping busy and keeping her muscles warm while she waited. She usually met her client, the overly chatty Mrs. Diane Mead, at two thirty. It was now three thirty, and no Mrs. Mead. Erin didn't mind if people were late, but hoped that they would at least call or send a message to let her know they were okay and if they were coming or not.

She stepped away from the punch bag and took off her gloves, drank a long gulp of water, and picked up her phone. Still no messages from Mrs. Mead.

Trying to make the time pass, she opened the Facebook app but saw only posts from former clients complaining about their kids and inappropriate jokes from people she didn't even remember friending. She closed it down again, fast.

She could text a friend. Maybe Erika or Julian? No, Erika was probably busy at work, and Julian had been so odd lately. Refusing to leave his house and claiming that she hit him with a telescope. It was a lie, of course. She wasn't the type to hit anyone. He, however, was the type to make things up for attention.

She sighed and wondered if she was getting too quick to judge people as she got older. First Mrs. Mead and now Julian, maybe that was why she socialized so little these days. She felt guilty. She'd always been the type to see the best in people, when had that changed?

She opened Twitter to see what was trending. There was nothing of real interest to her, only some scandal involving a politician and a debacle over an overly photoshopped magazine cover of a famous singer. She was ready to close it down when she saw a new tweet pop up from The_Apple_Core.

Yes, I'm procrastinating. Yes, I lack my usual discipline. Yes, I'm avoiding this heavy tomb of Norse fairy myths in front of me. Sigh.

Erin grinned and clicked into Isabella's profile to see what else she had tweeted. She noticed right away that the tweet she'd just seen wasn't there. She went back to her own Twitter feed. Nope, wasn't there. Apparently, Isabella changed her mind and deleted it.

Erin wasn't surprised. Isabella didn't seem the type to admit to failing to focus. Or that she was human and would procrastinate like everyone else, for that matter. Maybe she just wanted to talk to someone and that tweet was her way of showing it?

She opened her Skype app and typed a message.

BlackVelvetBitches: Don't think I didn't see that tweet before you removed it. :D Procrastinating like a boss, huh? You go with your bad self.

Erin wasn't sure if Isabella would reply or if she had gone back to researching. after a few seconds, a message popped up.

IsabellaMartinez1: Pardon? Oh, never mind. I'm glad I could amuse you, Miss Black. What are you doing online anyway? Shouldn't you be at work?

BlackVelvetBitches: I am. Sadly, the person I'm supposed to be training isn't. Just waiting for her to show up or call to cancel.

IsabellaMartinez1: I see. And if she cancels?

BlackVelvetBitches: Then I have some time to either workout or stand around talking to the cute girl in the gym's reception. ;-)

IsabellaMartinez1: Oh, so you'd use your precious free time for flirting?

Erin started typing the words *why? You fishing for some friendly flirting?* but then erased it and typed something more appropriate.

> **BlackVelvetBitches:** Hey, not all of us get the physical stuff at home. Some of us need to go hunting for it.

There was a pause before the reply came in, and once again, Erin wondered if she had said something stupid. Maybe that was even less appropriate than what she had first typed. She sighed, thinking she was just too tired to remember how to talk to people.

> **IsabellaMartinez1:**"The physical stuff"—is that what the cool kids are calling sex these days?

> **BlackVelvetBitches:** How would I know? I'm twenty-nine and certainly not cool.

> **IsabellaMartinez1:** You are, compared to me. I'm a few years older than you and thoroughly, unequivocally uncool.

Erin smiled at her screen.

> **BlackVelvetBitches:** Nah, you've got that cool, hipster coffee on tap. I'm just sleep-deprived, bored, sweaty, and standing around waiting for an old lady in a gym.

> **IsabellaMartinez1:** That does sound depressing. I, however, realized about an hour ago that I was discussing plots with my three-month old son, and he wasn't even awake. That must be a new low, surely?

Erin laughed and heard it echo against the walls of the corner. She looked around, a little embarrassed, but when she was sure that no one was paying attention to her, she went back to her phone.

> **BlackVelvetBitches:** Why don't you discuss it with me instead? I might not be more help than the little dude, but at least I'm awake.

> **IsabellaMartinez1:** Are you certain you are ready for what promises to be a thoroughly dull discourse?

Erin found herself smiling from ear to ear.

BlackVelvetBitches: Man, I love the way you talk. Did you swallow a dictionary AND grow up in Victorian London?

IsabellaMartinez1: Haha, very funny. No. I just had a mother who refused me dessert and playtime if I didn't speak and write properly. By the time I was an adult, the damage was done, and, ever since, I have found myself shying away from smileys, slang, unnecessary punctuation, and bad grammar. It annoys a lot of people, I'm afraid.

BlackVelvetBitches: Ah, the strict mother strikes again, huh? Well, I like the way you talk, so shy away from whatever the hell you want. Back to the point: hit me with your dullest discourse. I bet I'll stay awake.

IsabellaMartinez1: That's a very tempting offer, but His Highness is waking up, and it's time for our afternoon walk to the park.

Erin just barely managed to keep herself from groaning at the conversation being cut short.

BlackVelvetBitches: Damn, I can't compete with a guy who can charm people even if he is asleep and gassy. ;-)

IsabellaMartinez1: Excuse me, he isn't just gassy. The doctors also believe he has acid reflux!

Erin rolled her eyes but knew she was still smiling.

BlackVelvetBitches: Well, that's it, then. No one can resist that. :-D

IsabellaMartinez1: Hey, sarcastic and snarky remarks are MY trademark. And if you met Alberto, you would adore him as well.

BlackVelvetBitches: I'm sure I would. I mean, I'm not a baby person, but his mom is pretty awesome (so far), and he sounds like a cool guy. Does he need a personal trainer? ;-)

> **IsabellaMartinez1:** Sorry to disappoint, but I don't think his little muscles are ready for one of your shorts-splitting sessions.

Erin made a sound that was somewhere between a gasp and a scoff. This time, she definitely caught one of the old-timers looking over at her. She ignored him.

> **BlackVelvetBitches:** Hey! Low blow! That was a onetime thing, and only because Riley wears clothes that are tighter than most people's skin.

> **IsabellaMartinez1:** Whatever you say. Why don't you continue writing excuses, while I go to the park with my beautiful offspring? I'm sure I'll see you online tonight.

> **BlackVelvetBitches:** Sure. We'll meet up for some midnight coffee. You bring the belching baby, and I'll make the beverage.

> **IsabellaMartinez1:** I'm not going to dignify that with an answer. Speak to you soon, Miss Black.

> **BlackVelvetBitches:** See ya, Martinez.

Erin was just about to close down the chat window, when another message came in.

> **IsabellaMartinez1:** Oh, and for the record...don't assume someone is getting "the physical stuff" just because they're in a relationship. Have a good day, Erin.

Erin stared at the message with a confused frown. Why would Isabella make a point of hinting that she wasn't getting laid? Was she scolding Erin for making assumptions about people, or did she want Erin to know about her lack of sex life for some weird reason?

She sighed. If that perfect-in-every-way-MILF who lived with her boyfriend wasn't getting any—what chance did she have for sex with her crappy social skills and lack of energy? She wondered if maybe people had simply stopped doing it? No. If they had, Riley would be up in arms by now.

Suddenly, a whirlwind of flowery scarves over Lycra gym clothes came rushing toward her.

"I'm *so* sorry I'm late! Blame that nag of a woman opposite us, Carol Wiles. She stopped me to talk about her daughter's divorce and made me horribly delayed for everything."

Erin looked at Mrs. Mead and swallowed down any comment about calling to say she'd be late. Instead she smiled and said, "Not a problem. Let's hang those scarves up and get you on a treadmill."

Chapter 8

Coffee at Midnight

It was nearing midnight. Isabella had made a point of not opening Twitter or Skype all evening. She felt strangely nervous at the idea of speaking to Erin. What on earth had possessed her to mention her nonexistent sex life? Not that she had spelled it out, exactly, but it was certainly there in her statement. If you looked for it.

She closed her eyes and leant back in the chair. Alberto was asleep. That didn't surprise her. He'd been boisterous all day and had struggled to sleep during his naps; now he was making up for it. Isabella could only hope his little tummy would let him.

The room was quiet. Her blanket was draped over her legs, a cup of coffee cooled on the table next to her, and the writing app on her iPad boasted three new chapters for the first draft of her book.

It had been a successful evening, and Isabella was paying for it now. She had a wicked crick in her neck and tense shoulders from hunching over the iPad while correcting so many words unhelpfully changed by autocorrect.

She knew she should write on her shiny PC at her desk during the daytime, but today, she had been far too distracted by that brief chat with a certain friendly New Yorker. Besides, when the words started coming in hot and fast, it didn't matter if she was by a computer or in a dark room hunched over her tablet; she had to make the most of it and write. She could always edit the mistakes later.

But now, it was done, and she was back to thinking about Erin. She told herself that it was obvious she was fretting over what the woman thought about her simply because she wasn't socializing. Perhaps she should call an old a friend? Maybe even call Marie back and ask if she was taking any work trips down to Florida? *No, I'm not that desperate*, she thought and scrunched up her nose.

She just had to stop overthinking her interactions with Erin and focus on having fun. That was all it was, some fun chat to make the hours of the sleepless nights run faster.

A little voice in her head pointed out that Alberto was sleeping right now, and by that reasoning, she should be too. If talking to Erin was just a way to pass time, why didn't she skip speaking with her tonight and get some sleep instead?

Nevertheless, Isabella couldn't bring herself to do that. It was nearing midnight, and she was sitting ready, cup of coffee on the table, app opened on the tablet. Staring at her screen. Waiting for Erin.

The seconds ticked by. Then there was a green dot by Erin's name, and Isabella typed a quick greeting.

IsabellaMartinez1: Hello Erin.

The reply came in right away, satisfying Isabella's need for affirmation.

BlackVelvetBitches: Fancy meeting you here, Martinez. :)

IsabellaMartinez1: Well, I heard this is where you go for midnight coffee.

Reminded of the drink next to her, Isabella blew on the hot liquid and had her first sip.

BlackVelvetBitches: Does that mean you have java at the ready?

IsabellaMartinez1: Java? Who says "java" these days? Are you living in an old film noir?

BlackVelvetBitches: :-D Maybe I am. Sometimes, late at night, New York certainly feels like it could be the setting for an old, hardboiled film noir, y'know? I just need a smoking gun and a dame.

Isabella was relieved that Erin knew what film noir was, unlike Richard, who had little interest in pop culture.

IsabellaMartinez1: Searching for a femme fatale? That could be dangerous, Miss Black.

BlackVelvetBitches: That (and caffeine poisoning) happen to be my ways of living dangerously. :-D

IsabellaMartinez1: Ah, I see. Does that mean that you date...for a lack of a better term..."bad girls?"

BlackVelvetBitches: Honestly? I haven't dated for ages. Last woman I was serious about... Well, let's just say that she screwed me over royally. I guess I didn't feel it was worth the hassle after that.

Alberto squirmed and whined a little, and Isabella prayed he wouldn't wake up now. This was not a point in the conversation where she could just disappear for five minutes.

She snuck up and twisted the little key that started the mobile above his head. The unicorns slowly turned, and the quiet, slow waltz soothed Alberto. He gave one last squirm and then relaxed back into deep sleep. She sat back down and picked up the iPad.

IsabellaMartinez1: I'm so sorry to hear that. Might I ask what happened? Or perhaps you don't want to talk about it?

BlackVelvetBitches: No, it's fine. It's been over a year, so the wounds should pretty much be healed by now. Katie had, well, HAS, some issues. She had an ever weirder childhood than me, and let's just say that it shows.

Isabella frowned. She wanted more information, but she wasn't the type to pry or push people to talk. While she debated whether she should change the topic or not, another message came in from Erin.

BlackVelvetBitches: I don't want to bore you with some long sob story, so I'll just boil it down to the fact that it ended with her stealing most of my money. Oh, and leaving me with a note saying that she had to go find her mother and that I deserved better than her. I haven't heard from her since. She updates her Facebook sometimes though. Last time I checked, she had found her mom in some small town in Maine, which was nice to hear.

"Nice to hear?" Isabella said in appalled surprise.

She realized that she had spoken out loud and drew a sigh of relief when she saw that Alberto hadn't woken up. It stunned her that Erin could be so gracious to someone who had run out on her and stolen her money not that long ago.

IsabellaMartinez1: It's very big of you to be happy for her after what she did to you.

BlackVelvetBitches: Nah, it's probably just me being a sap. She meant a helluva lot to me. So no matter how pissed off or disappointed I am in how she left me, I'm glad she found what she was looking for. It was for the best anyway. There were waaaay too many misunderstandings and arguments when we were together. She was always pissed off, and I've got this tendency to run and hide when things get serious. Not a good combo.

Isabella looked deep into her dark coffee and sighed.

IsabellaMartinez1: Relationships are terribly complicated, aren't they?

BlackVelvetBitches: Yeah. Screw relationships. Give me a chat with a woman I've never met any day. :-D

Isabella arched an eyebrow, a smirk replacing her scowl.

IsabellaMartinez1: Are you saying that I'm a substitute for a relationship?

BlackVelvetBitches: What? Shit, no! That's not what I meant! I mean, I know you're in a relationship and probably not into women, so I would never hit on you!

Isabella gave a subdued scoff. She'd quite like to be hit on. She missed the thrill of being attracted to someone and having that person be attracted to her in return. The occurrence of that was such a rare thing for her, and when it did strike, it was never long-lived.

IsabellaMartinez1: Relax, Miss Black. I didn't think you were trying to seduce me.

She wondered if she should address the issue of her not being into women. The truth was that she'd always been curious and had been attracted to a few women throughout her life. But it had always stayed at just that. Either she'd been in a relationship with a man, or she was focusing all her energy on her studies or her work. Pursuing lovers had always been pretty low on her list of priorities.

As far as she knew, she'd never been hit on by another woman. Unless some of the friendly gestures she had assumed were platonic had been meant as flirting, and she just hadn't realized. Society didn't seem to focus much on teaching you to romantically interact with people of your own sex.

If a man smiled at her, sat very close, and kept eye contact throughout a conversation, she would probably say he was interested in her. If a woman did the same...well she was either extremely friendly or slightly socially awkward.

Or so Isabella had thought. For the first time in her life, she wondered if some of the women she had dismissed as friends because they were too intense, had actually been attracted to her. Why had she never stopped to think about this before?

Erin wasn't replying. Isabella frowned, as she tried to figure out why. Was Erin trying to find a way to continue the conversation but failing? Was she embarrassed?

Isabella decided to help in any way she could, even if it meant being more candid than she was comfortable with. She took a deep breath and started typing.

IsabellaMartinez1: Sorry, I got lost in thought there. I was just realizing that I had always been curious about being with a woman but never been hit on by one. However, maybe that's because I was so stuck in...what's the word...heteronormative

(?) thinking. Maybe women have been flirting with me, and I just never realized?

Isabella could see the little pen on her screen, signifying that Erin was typing. Then it disappeared again. There was a long moment's wait, and then the pen appeared once more.

She wondered again what Erin was thinking. What had she written and then deleted? Was she annoyed that Isabella had lived her life without accounting for gay women in her life, or was she perhaps still embarrassed over the misunderstanding?

BlackVelvetBitches: Human interaction, it's all so freakin' weird. I spend so much time wondering if a woman would be okay with me flirting that by the time I've figured it out, she's gone! I guess that's why gay clubs are so nice, you go in there, and you know that even if the women aren't into women (which is rare) at least they don't mind being hit on by women. And it's why I like the Internet. A lot of people will at least hint to their sexual orientation somewhere in their bio. Well, at least if they are LGBTQIA+.

IsabellaMartinez1: I'd never thought about that. Well, mark me down as not offended if women hit on me. If I even realize they are hitting on me. Not that anything more could happen, of course. I have Richard.

She had added that last bit as an afterthought. Maybe that went without saying, but she didn't want Erin to think she was looking for someone to flirt with.

BlackVelvetBitches: Wow, this got serious. :-D Let's change the topic. Lemme tell you a joke a client told me at work last week.

IsabellaMartinez1: I'm not hugely into jokes. But go ahead.

BlackVelvetBitches: Why do bees hum?

It took a while before Isabella realized that she was expected to reply.

IsabellaMartinez1: I don't know.

BlackVelvetBitches: Because they can't remember lyrics. Ba-bom tssh!

IsabellaMartinez1: That was awful. Painfully awful. And was that supposed to be a rim shot at the end?

BlackVelvetBitches: Yep. And I don't know what you're complaining about; I'm great at dad jokes. Speaking of parents... how's your lil' man?

IsabellaMartinez1: Blissfully unaware of how complicated being an adult can be. He is sleeping surprisingly soundly. He had an active day, so he needs his sleep.

BlackVelvetBitches: Well, one of us three should get some sleep. Go Alberto!

Isabella looked at the little boy through the bars of his crib. His small chest was moving fast with his breaths, and she could see that his mouth was slightly open.

Her heart clenched. He was the most beautiful thing she had ever seen. Without filtering her thoughts, she turned back to Skype and just typed what she was feeling.

IsabellaMartinez1: I wish I could show him to you. He's sleeping so peacefully, and he's so sweet that it breaks my heart.

BlackVelvetBitches: Hmm. Well, I mean, you can. All you gotta do is call me and switch on the camera. Maybe seeing someone sleep like a baby will make my stupid brain wanna sleep too.

Isabella hesitated. Was Erin just being nice? She had mentioned that she wasn't much of a baby person, hadn't she? But Alberto looked so perfect, and he was the thing she was proudest of. It would help Erin understand her and her choices if she could see him.

IsabellaMartinez1: All right. Just for a moment and then I'll hang up. I don't want to bore you.

BlackVelvetBitches: I'm sure you won't. Come on, show me your little womb nugget.

Isabella scoffed but couldn't help laughing a little.

IsabellaMartinez1: Not if you refer to him as that!

BlackVelvetBitches: Fine, fine. Show me the little prince charming.

Isabella, still smiling, pushed the button to video call Erin. It was going to be a one-sided video call again, and that made Isabella remember the last time, when she had shown her the desk and then made the stupid faux pas of turning the camera on her unkempt self. She wouldn't be making that mistake tonight.

As the call connected, Erin spoke right away. She whispered hello, but the whisper was so over the top that it sounded like really bad acting. It was far, far too loud.

Isabella's smile grew, and if she hadn't been forced to be quiet to keep from waking Alberto, she would have laughed and mocked Erin mercilessly for that ridiculous attempt at a whisper.

Suddenly, she realized that the camera was on but pointed just at the floor. She whispered a greeting back, much quieter than Erin had, and then stood up and pointed the iPad at Alberto. She walked closer, so that Erin could see the details of his little face in the glow of his night-light.

With maternal pride, she watched him and wished that she could narrate for Erin, point out the perfect, petite nose, and the stunning eyes. Maybe even the little cut on his chin where he scratched himself with one of his tiny fingernails that morning and, of course, the little mouth that would nibble at her shoulder when he was hungry.

Instead, she heard Erin theatre whisper, "Okay, he *is* really cute. Dude has hair! Like, hair that you can see. Is that common?"

Isabella had to keep from laughing again and whispered back, "Yes, he's inherited my dark, thick hair, and I'm proud to say that he has much more hair than the other children in our baby group."

"Baby group?"

"Yes. It's a group that..." Isabella broke off because Alberto started to fidget, kicking his little feet before settling down again.

"I'm going to hang up and type to you again. I don't want to wake him."

"Of course," Erin replied.

Isabella hung up, feeling rude for not saying goodbye even though the conversation would obviously continue. She started typing.

> **IsabellaMartinez1:** Once a month we attend a group that is moms with babies. I met most of them in Lamaze class, and then we just carried on meeting at the house of a woman named Debbie. We basically talk about the woes and perks of having a baby and then split up. Or, to be exact, I leave. After that, the subjects tend to drift to what everyone's husband is doing and general gossip. I don't have time for that.

> **BlackVelvetBitches:** Don't have time for it, or don't have patience for it? ;-)

> **IsabellaMartinez1:** Both. I go home and write or clean the house. Those are much better ways for me to spend my time.

> **BlackVelvetBitches:** I'm not gonna disagree with you. I'm not very social these days.

> **IsabellaMartinez1:** These days? You haven't always been the introvert that your Twitter bio proclaims you to be?

> **BlackVelvetBitches:** Nope! Believe it or not, I used to be pretty social until my late teens. Then something changed, I suppose. I started to dread going to parties and finding that I got really tired whenever I spent a lot of time with people, even if I liked them. So now, I don't hang out with that many people.

> **IsabellaMartinez1:** There's nothing wrong with that. I'm more introverted than extroverted myself. But you do socialize sometimes, right?

> **BlackVelvetBitches:** I have three friends I still meet up with occasionally: Luke, Julian, and Erika. Oh, and I suppose you can call Riley a friend too. Other than that, it's just me and my guns.

Isabella wasn't sure which of her two emotions was strongest at that moment, the shock or the distaste.

IsabellaMartinez1: Guns?

BlackVelvetBitches: Yeah, weight lifting, boxing, the occasional Bikram yoga session, and so on. Builds muscles all over, but I'm most proud of my guns.

Isabella felt utterly confused. And then it all cleared up in an instant.

IsabellaMartinez1: Oh, you mean your arms! I thought you meant actual firearms.

BlackVelvetBitches: Nah, I mean the gun show that is currently happening in my pajama top. :-D

IsabellaMartinez1: You're in your pajamas?

BlackVelvetBitches: Well, technically it's a pair of boxer shorts and a hoodie, but I use it for pajamas on cold nights like tonight.

Isabella shivered without knowing why. She ignored it and typed back.

IsabellaMartinez1: I see. So, did seeing Alberto work? Did it make you feel inclined to sleep?

BlackVelvetBitches: You know what? It kinda did. Or, well, something did. I might get to sleep before four! That would be good, because I have my first client at nine thirty, and it's this really meticulous guy, so being less sleep deprived than usual would be awesome.

IsabellaMartinez1: How much sleep do you normally get per night?

As she waited for Erin's reply, she noticed that Alberto was fidgeting and making little sniffling noises. She decoded the movements; he was hurting and about to wake up. No musical mobile could fix this.

IsabellaMartinez1: Sorry. Alberto's waking up. I'll try to be back when he has calmed.

Alberto cried and cried. Isabella ended up spending a long time rubbing his tummy and his back. In the end, she had to give him a teaspoon of a potent anti-colic syrup the doctor had prescribed for nights when his stomach was worse than usual.

She sat down and fed him while clicking the iPad to see if Erin had come back. There was a single message:

BlackVelvetBitches: Okay. I'm bringing the laptop to bed. If I don't reply later on, I have somehow managed to sleep.

When Alberto was full and the medicine had kicked in, he finally went back to sleep. Isabella placed him in his crib with a soft kiss on his downy hair.

She sat back in the chair and noticed that she was smiling. In her head, she could hear a sweet, female voice whisper, "Okay, he *is* really cute," far too loudly.

She realized how much she enjoyed Erin genuine honesty. There was a sweetness and down-to-earth quality to Erin, which reminded her of what she had first been attracted to in Richard.

The difference was… Well, there were a lot of differences. But the one that seemed to stand out the most to her right now was that Erin had another side. That side had seen misery and lived through it. Richard's childhood had been lovely and normal, something which must have shaped him just as Erin's and her own negative childhood experiences had shaped them.

Erin was so much easier for Isabella to relate to. And far too easy to talk to. Isabella worried that if they kept talking, she would spill her whole life story. All her fears, and dreams too. But then, there was a relief in that.

She picked up her iPad.

IsabellaMartinez1: The prince is sleeping. Are you?

She waited while checking her Twitter and a news app, but there was no reply from Erin.

Isabella hoped that meant that she had fallen asleep. She tried to imagine her curled up next to her laptop in her boxer shorts and her hoodie. She found herself hoping that Erin had pulled the covers or blankets over herself. If it was such a cold night in New York, she'd need to be covered and cozy.

She dismissed the thought. It was too intimate for someone she didn't really know. Not yet anyway. But she was getting to know her, wasn't she? Maybe even better than she had known Richard when she'd called to tell him that she was keeping the baby and wanted them to try being a family.

The realization stunned her. Could that be true? Granted, she'd spent more time with Richard, but most of it had involved making love or eating a nice meal together, never just…talking.

Growing weary and wishing not to be the only one still awake, Isabella drew the cashmere blanket over herself and relaxed back into the plush armchair, hoping for sleep.

Chapter 9

Waiting Brings Unwanted Thoughts

ERIN HAD FALLEN ASLEEP IN the end, but it had taken a while. She'd felt strangely tired and calm, as if that near-sleep feeling she'd been chasing for months had finally slowed enough to let her catch it. But she'd still kept herself up a little longer, marveling at how affected she was by knowing that Isabella was bisexual. Or at least bi-curious. She'd gone out of her way to say that she didn't mind women hitting on her. But, then, she'd also pointed out that it wouldn't go anywhere because of Richard.

This wasn't news to Erin. She knew Isabella wasn't on the market. Nonetheless, Isabella would consider being with a woman. The idea made butterflies take flight in Erin's stomach. She just couldn't help it.

Then there was the kid. She hadn't been lying when she said he was cute. She didn't lie, not unless she really, really had to. But she hadn't in this case. He was adorable in that alien-looking baby way. So innocent and vulnerable. That wispy tuft of dark hair and his little mouth, open in an O as he took his deep, sleeping breaths.

Yeah, he was a charmer, just like his mom. Erin could say that after only having seen him once. Or maybe she liked him because of how Isabella adored him? Despite the fact that Isabella had been whispering, that melted-chocolate voice turned even warmer when she was talking about her kid.

When Erin's alarm went off in the morning, she woke, shocked to realized that she felt well rested. She couldn't even remember any dreams. The whole night had just been a heavy, soft blanket of refreshing sleep.

She got up and had some oatmeal and coffee, before dressing and heading off to work. While she was on the subway, struggling to get her MetroCard into her stupidly small pocket, she remembered what she'd said to Isabella about her current lack of social life.

It made her wonder if she should call someone and go out for coffee or a drink or two. When she was above ground and heading for the doors of Nash's Gym, she sent off a quick text to Erika, her Swedish friend living in Brooklyn. She hadn't spoken to her in ages. *It must be at least three months since either of us even checked up on each other.*

A reply came in right away; Erika was probably bored at work and checking her phone. They decided on coffee at Erin's the next day. Saturday. Conveniently.

Ten minutes later, Erin greeted her first client and listened to him complain about sore muscles from last time, all the while wondering if meeting up with Erika would work as well as chatting with Isabella had. Would it also make her feel happier? Would it make her sleep better? Or was Isabella about more than merely curing her loneliness? She dismissed the thoughts and focused on work.

After coming home from work and eating a healthy dinner, Erin was ready to tackle the evening. It was amazing how much more rested she still felt; those extra hours of sleep had really done her good.

She decided to watch a movie and, in a fit of nostalgia, popped *Back to the Future* into the DVD player. However, she found herself glancing toward her laptop over on the table.

Her thoughts ran away with her. When would Isabella be online tonight? Was it too early now? Did she, Richard, and the lil' man eat dinner early or late? Was Isabella writing?

In the end, she picked up her phone to check her apps. Nope. Isabella wasn't online.

She sighed and tried to focus back on the movie but continued to struggle against the thoughts of what Isabella might be doing. Was she sitting with Richard on a couch watching TV? They didn't seem very close, but then they did live together and had a kid together, so they were probably hanging out at night.

When the movie ended, Erin was almost relieved. Trying to focus had been annoying. She considered going for a run to clear her head. Instead, she found herself at her laptop.

Isabella still wasn't online. Erin couldn't help it; she went to message her on Skype. She saw the last message sent.

IsabellaMartinez1: The prince is sleeping. Are you?

Ridiculous as it was, a cold feeling of loss came over her when she saw the words. She would've gotten more time with Isabella if she hadn't fallen asleep last night. She weighed the extra sleep she got against more time talking with Isabella and found that the much-needed sleep won out. But not by much, and she was sure it was only because she'd speak to Isabella soon.

She decided to write a response Isabella could pick up when she came online.

BlackVelvetBitches: I was sleeping, yeah. Like a baby! Staring at your womb nugget snoozing clearly worked. ;-)

Erin sat back and smiled contentedly. She was willing to bet that re-using the womb nugget thing would make Isabella put down what she was doing to come and tell her off.

She turned out to be right. The little green dot that signaled Isabella's presence online popped up next to her name.

IsabellaMartinez1: Firstly, we have discussed the use of the term womb nugget, and I made my opinion clear. Use it again, and I will send you a picture of the contents of his diaper. Secondly, I am glad you got some sleep. I am just about to give Alberto his bath, then I'll put him to bed and come online. Will you still be here?

Erin blew out a long breath. Of course she would. There was no point in kidding herself. She would wait for hours, just for a brief chat with this woman. Hell, hadn't she been waiting for hours already?

BlackVelvetBitches: Yep. I'll be right here, Martinez.

She'd written, "when am I getting my bath?" at the end, just as a joke, then realized how flirty it sounded and deleted it before sending the message.

Erin got up to walk around and stretch her legs. She went to look out the window. There were some people outside the Irish bar; two of them were smoking, and the others were talking animatedly.

Erin was relieved to not be out there with them. Not just because she was an introvert and social interaction drained her, but because she wouldn't switch her dingy little apartment, with its laptop connected to Isabella's world, for anything else in the universe. All she wanted she had right here. "Except a dog. Stupid landlord and his stupid rules," she muttered to herself.

She went to make coffee and listened to the quiet hum of her laptop. Maybe it wasn't all she needed. What would it be like if, instead of appearing on the screen, Isabella walked into this room? Erin's mind drifted into daydreams about that. What would Isabella look like? What would she say? What would she smell like?

She shivered. She felt as if she had crossed some invisible line. Isabella had a life in Florida. A partner, a child, and a budding career as a writer. All Erin was to her was someone harmless to chat to, someone to have a brief conversation with and then forget about.

The fact that Erin imagined her here, in her intimate, little home, somehow felt like she was doing something bad. But why? It wasn't like she was imagining Isabella in her bed, just in her home. Just walking into the room, sighing with a tired smile, and saying, "He's finally asleep. Would you make some coffee, Erin? I'm utterly exhausted."

Erin shivered again. This was even worse. What was she doing, and why did it make her feel so guilty? She groaned. *God, am I really that lonely?*

Why did these imaginings make her feel like she was trespassing on Isabella's life?

This was all too complicated. She slammed her finger onto the power button on the coffeemaker and shut her eyes, focusing as hard as possible on what dog she would get if she could have one and how she'd go jogging with it.

Slowly, the unwanted thoughts dissipated. By the time the coffee had poured through the filter, Erin was relaxed again. She opened a cabinet and picked up a peanut butter protein bar. She read the contents. Way too much sugar. She'd have to switch to unsweetened ones. One day. Maybe. For now, these bars were a better option than going out to buy a bear claw or munching down a plate of waffles.

She ate her bar and sipped her coffee as she watched the street below. As always, she could hear distant music, people shouting at each other, and the constant hum of traffic. Somewhere, a vehicle beeped long and hard at someone else.

Erin was trying hard to keep her thoughts clear from finding ways to ask Isabella about her dreams, hopes, and fears. She was also trying not to think of ways to ask Isabella for pictures of herself or to turn on the camera again.

She's not yours to fall in love with, pal.

She wasn't sure how long she had been standing there with a half-empty coffee cup and a scrunched-up wrapper when her laptop pinged, nearly giving her whiplash, she turned toward it so fast. Erin hurried over and slammed her cup down on the table, pushing the wrapper into the lukewarm coffee.

> **IsabellaMartinez1:** The young gentleman is now clean, fed, and asleep. I am just about to go down and fetch some coffee. Are you here and free to chat for a while?

Erin slowly counted to five, to not seem like she was waiting so eagerly, then replied.

> **BlackVelvetBitches:** Sure! I've had my coffee, but I can join you for another cup in a while. What about Richard?

> **IsabellaMartinez1:** What about him?

> **BlackVelvetBitches:** It's still pretty early. Don't you want to hang out with him?

> **IsabellaMartinez1:** Not really. I'm certain he has things to do.

Despite the curt tone in that message, Erin was smiling. Isabella was choosing her company over Richard's. Even if that probably said more about

Isabella's feelings for her boyfriend than it did about Isabella's feelings for her, she couldn't help but feel that she had somehow…won.

> **BlackVelvetBitches:** Fair enough. His loss is my gain. Go get your coffee, woman! I'll be here.

> **IsabellaMartinez1:** Thank you for the kind sentiment, Miss Black. I'll be right back.

Erin, still smiling, gave a happy sigh and waited patiently for Isabella's return.

Chapter 10

There's Richard...and Then There is Erin

WALKING DOWN THE STAIRS QUIETLY, Isabella thought about those words. "His loss is my gain." Was that how it was? Was this time that she was looking forward to spending with Erin time she should be spending with Richard? She knew the answer before she had even finished the thought; of course it was.

Right now, Richard was lying on the sofa, eating sunflower seeds and texting his best friend while half watching some show about archery.

While she, well, she was going to spend the last hours of the day talking to a lesbian in New York. No, thinking about Erin like that felt...wrong. She was so much more than that. So much more interesting than that.

Isabella scolded herself. She knew nothing about Erin, and that was exactly what this was all about. It was the writer in her who'd seen an interesting character and wanted to know more about her. *Yes, that must be it*, she managed to convince herself.

Well, almost convinced herself.

She hurried down to make her coffee. In the kitchen, she stared at the door to the living room where Richard was watching TV. She could hear the muffled narration of the show through the wood. She could open that door, go in and lie down on the sofa, cuddle in his arms, or lie her head on his chest. She wondered if that would make him happy or uncomfortable.

He always acted as though anything she did, anything she wanted, was fine. But surely, he must have a preference. She thought about the chaste kisses he placed on her cheeks and the friendly claps on the back. Were those for her benefit or his?

Perhaps his calm indifference was just a mask. When they'd decided to try and be a family, she'd asked him not to suffocate her. No, that wasn't quite right; she'd demanded it from him. And he'd promised. Maybe this was his way of ensuring he kept that promise. Did he want more? Did he need more from her?

The thoughts and questions hurt. Guilt lodged in her throat, making it hard to swallow.

She made the coffee and thought about Alberto instead. He always made things feel better. She thought about his chubby hands that looked like doll hands screwed on to his soft little arms, thanks to the crease on his wrist. Those hands mapped as much of her face as they could reach while she breastfed him.

How could a little person make everything so warm and magical? She'd never thought she would be a mother. Now, it was the only thing she knew for certain that she wanted to be.

She watched the coffee start to trickle and wished it would hurry up. She wanted to go upstairs to Alberto and to...well, to Erin.

Finally, clutching her coffee, she started to walk upstairs, but the guilt was still there, and she stopped halfway up. As usual, anger was her first response. She cursed under her breath. Then she strode back down, put her coffee on the kitchen counter, and walked into the living room.

"Richard? Sorry to disturb you. I just wanted to say good night, as I'm going upstairs to sit with Alberto."

"Okay. Good night. Are you going to try and do some writing up there?"

Isabella hesitated. "No. Actually, I've started chatting with this woman in New York."

Richard looked confused, and Isabella realized that she probably looked tense or strange. She made an effort to look normal and smiled at him. She didn't feel guilty because she was doing anything wrong by speaking to Erin. She felt guilty because she knew she was choosing Erin's company over Richard's. And she had just told him.

She searched his face for signs of him being offended or disappointed. But there was nothing but a relaxed smile now.

"I'm glad you've made a new friend. You spend too much time alone, Isabella. You can't spend all your time with Alberto. Have fun!"

Isabella found herself clenching her hands into fists at her sides. She couldn't understand why he didn't ask questions about this woman or ask her to come watch TV with him instead. Well, maybe she could understand it. Was he so disinterested in her, in her life, that it didn't matter to him? Or was he just so wrapped up in his own little world, his own friends and interests, the parts of his life that she wasn't in, that it didn't matter to him? Did the reason behind his disinterest really matter when the result was the same?

Still, to her shame, she felt relieved. She wondered what she would have done if he had asked her to stay with him? Deep down, she knew the answer. She'd have found an excuse to leave. She didn't want to spend time with him, and he didn't seem to want to spend time with her. What did that say about their relationship?

"Yes, it's nice to talk to someone new and to tell her about Alberto. Anyway, I better go before my coffee gets cold. Have a good night. I'll see you tomorrow."

She walked over, and this time, it was she who kissed his cheek. He smelled faintly of cologne and something nature-ish, something that felt foreign to her city senses. He smiled at her.

"Thanks. Try to get some sleep as well. It can't be good for your back to sit in that chair all night."

Isabella winced a little. "I know. My back is quite sore, if I'm honest. Don't worry, I'll probably stretch it out with that old Pilates DVD I have somewhere. Anyway, I always lie flat on the bed when Alberto and I have our daytime naps."

"I know. Nevertheless, you have to be careful, Isabella. You only get one body in this life."

She searched his face again. He spoke about her body so dispassionately, as if it wasn't something he had wanted and loved at one point.

"I'll be careful. Don't stay up too late, or you'll be tired in the morning. Good night, Richard."

When he nodded and smiled, she gave him another peck on the cheek. The guilt was still there as she walked back into the kitchen, but it had lessened considerably. A thrill went through her, as she thought of her coffee and her chat with Erin. She took her mug and forced herself to walk upstairs at a normal speed and not hurry to her iPad. When she finally reached the nursery, she caressed Alberto's chubby cheek and then sat down quickly.

IsabellaMartinez1: I'm back.

BlackVelvetBitches: Really? I thought you were Isabella?

IsabellaMartinez1: Oh, very funny.

BlackVelvetBitches: That's nothin'. Listen to this...What's at the bottom of the ocean and shivers?

IsabellaMartinez1: I don't know.

BlackVelvetBitches: A nervous wreck. :-D

IsabellaMartinez1: Erin, that was abysmal. I'd like those thirty seconds of my life back, please.

BlackVelvetBitches: Fine, back to serious stuff. I was just thinking that I've told you about my job and a little about my shitty childhood. But I don't know anything about you. Tell me about Isabella Martinez. Start at the beginning. What was baby Isabella like? Having seen your kid, I bet you were cute as hell.

Isabella was biting her lower lip while smiling. Why shouldn't she share a little? What could it hurt to try? Just this once. She summoned her courage and the energy to rail against her own instincts, then blew out a breath and started typing.

IsabellaMartinez1: I don't know about cute. I was a precocious, know-it-all young girl, who loved horses and teasing her younger sister. Have I told you about Marie?

BlackVelvetBitches: No, I don't think so.

IsabellaMartinez1: Marie is my sister—well, technically, a foster sister. But more importantly, she's a real pain in the neck. Remind me to tell you more about her later.

BlackVelvetBitches: Okay, will do. Tell me more about that horse-loving brat. ;-)

IsabellaMartinez1: Excuse me, I did not say "brat." Keep your judgments to yourself. Now, let's see. Where should I pick up from? Well, other than Marie, my family consists of my mother, Judith, and my father, Alberto. My father, whom I tend to still call Daddy—and I don't expect any jokes about that—is a wonderful man. He's kind, intelligent, warm, humble, and as brilliant in English as he is in his native Spanish.

BlackVelvetBitches: Alberto? You named your son after your dad, huh?

IsabellaMartinez1: Yes. I hope the name will just be one of the many things he inherits from his grandfather. Hopefully, he grows up to be a little more independent than Daddy, though.

BlackVelvetBitches: How so?

Isabella found herself squirming in her seat. It was time to talk about her again.

IsabellaMartinez1: For all of Daddy's positive traits, he has one weakness. Mother. If she tells him to jump off a cliff, he will only stop to ask if she wants him to survive the fall or not. For some reason, he adores her, despite her many unpleasant traits. He always tells the story of how as a young man, he went into a library to study. There he ran into this all-American girl with flawless porcelain skin and a sharp wit. He fell head over heels in love with her. He never believed she would even look twice at him. But she not only looked at him again, a year later, she agreed to marry him.

BlackVelvetBitches: You know, I like the way you tell stories. I feel like I'm reading a book or something. Anyway, sorry, that was a side note. It sounds nice to have parents who are so in love.

Isabella liked the compliment but ignored it. She had to continue explaining about her mother. If she paused now, she would stop completely and bury it all again. She had to get it out quickly and succinctly, purge the poison.

> **IsabellaMartinez1:** Well, it would have been nice if his adoration of her hadn't meant he let her get away with everything and if that fact didn't have dire consequences for me, and later for Marie, as well. No matter what Mother did, he never intervened or spoke up. Not even those times Mother locked me in the basement all night for sneaking out after curfew, or for disobeying her orders. All he did was make me my favorite breakfast the next day and tell me that my mother only wanted to help me.

> **BlackVelvetBitches:** Shit. Your mom was a real piece of work.

> **IsabellaMartinez1:** Yes. I know I shouldn't complain to someone who had to grow up without her parents, but I think it will help you to understand me, if you understand more about my mother. She came from nothing, and through hard work and marrying well, she's ended up very rich and powerful. I suppose, she forced the carefree, horse-loving girl out of me very quickly and taught me to be as cold and calculating as she had to be.

Isabella couldn't stand anymore right now. She led the conversation away from her mother and into her current life, but still she refused to guard herself or clam up. She was surprised to find that she wanted to talk, needed to talk. She skirted over her education, her career, and her fight up the ladder to the position of CEO. How she had done things she wasn't proud of to achieve that.

> **BlackVelvetBitches:** What do you mean "things you aren't proud of?"

Isabella frowned. She had to draw the line somewhere. She'd already told Erin about the coldness she'd inherited from her mother; she felt too ashamed to demonstrate examples of it. Besides, maybe she'd shared enough for one night. She didn't want to scare Erin off completely.

IsabellaMartinez1: It's nothing big. I'll tell you another time, perhaps. I'm starting to get a bit tired now. Aren't you tired?

BlackVelvetBitches: Yeah. We should be asleep. We're too old and have too many responsibilities to be up all night. :-D

IsabellaMartinez1: You're right, of course. Nevertheless, I'm afraid I wouldn't get any sleep, even if I tried.

BlackVelvetBitches: Yeah, same here. It doesn't matter how tired I am or how late it is. I'm an insomniac, just the same. So screw all of that. Tell me more about you instead, about grown-up you. What do you like to do when you're not writing, burping a baby, or harassing actors on Twitter?

IsabellaMartinez1: I certainly did not harass him. I only told him some truths he needed to hear.

BlackVelvetBitches: Sure. :-D Whatever you say. Still, tell me about what you like to do.

Isabella rubbed her stiff neck as she considered that.

IsabellaMartinez1: I've always liked to travel. We traveled a lot when I was little. Mother wanted me to see the "old cities," as she called them. So we went to Paris, Moscow, London, Alexandria, and a few other places. As a child, traveling with my parents... It wasn't always fun, or easy. But I've made up for that by enjoying my own travels as an adult. My favorite was Shanghai. Before Alberto was born, I tended to go back there whenever I felt like I had time for a holiday.

BlackVelvetBitches: Wow. That makes my road trips around the state seem like walks around the block. :(

IsabellaMartinez1: Trust me, you'd be better off traveling around New York on your own, than standing in a concert hall in Vienna while Judith Martinez scolds you in front of a crowd for smiling at a passing boy.

BlackVelvetBitches: Why the hell weren't you allowed to smile at him?

IsabellaMartinez1: Because we didn't know him, and he looked "unwashed and uncouth"—her words not mine, obviously.

BlackVelvetBitches: You're right. I could smile at as many unwashed people as I wanted on my trips. Now, that's my definition of freedom.

Isabella stifled a laugh, making sure not to wake Alberto.

Soon it was past midnight, and Isabella was amazed that time had gone so fast. She faintly recalled hearing Richard sneak past the door to go to bed, and she knew that Alberto had a few close calls and almost woke up, but it all happened somewhere in the periphery of her consciousness.

Talking to Erin was what had mattered. Letting the words flow as they wished. Not controlling them to make sure she wasn't saying too much or trying to arrange them to look good in a manuscript or work memo. She had just relaxed and…talked.

IsabellaMartinez1: God, look at how I've rambled on about myself. I'm so sorry, Erin.

BlackVelvetBitches: Are you kidding me? Don't apologize. I'm so happy you told me all about this. Your life is really interesting. I want to hear more.

Isabella felt a smile forming. Erin wanted to hear more? After all that she had disclosed, after all the parts of herself she'd just let Erin see, she still wanted more?

Isabella had just broken every social rule her mother had forcibly instilled in her. She hadn't been on her guard and kept up appearances, she hadn't analyzed her companion before being open with her, and she hadn't made mental notes about what she had disclosed.

As it hit her just how much she had divulged, she began to feel uncomfortable. Erin had the upper hand now. With a shake of her head, she reminded herself that Erin didn't seem to be the sort of person who would ever use personal information against someone. Still, she felt an urgent need to stop before this went any further. Frowning, she tried to find an excuse to leave.

> **IsabellaMartinez1:** I think Alberto might be waking up. Maybe we should call it a night?

> **BlackVelvetBitches:** Aww, do we have to? Yeah, I guess I should try for some sleep. Maybe it'll be like last night, and I'll actually manage some snoozing. :-D On one condition, though: you meet me here tomorrow. If you can't make it before, then at least for some midnight coffee. ;-)

Isabella's frown smoothed a little.

> **IsabellaMartinez1:** Only if you promise me that we will talk more about you then. You owe me some background.

> **BlackVelvetBitches:** Deal. G'night, Ms. Writer. I hope you get some sleep.

> **IsabellaMartinez1:** You too, Erin.

She meant it. Erin deserved the best of everything, and that certainly included sleep.

Chapter 11

Erika

ERIN CLOSED THE LID OF the laptop with a smile on her face. Isabella Martinez was no longer just a stranger she had met on the Internet; at least, it didn't feel like it anymore. Her mind was reeling with everything she had learned. She'd just taken a crash course called Isabella Martinez 101.

She knew she should try to sleep, since she was meeting Erika tomorrow for coffee. But how could she sleep? She felt like some sugary energy drink was blitzing through her veins.

Needing to calm down, she returned to the street view from her window. She remembered reading, somewhere, that when we made a new friend we really liked, the same chemicals flooded our brains as when we fell in romantic love, just in a smaller amount.

Leaning against the cold glass of the window, she bit her lip and wondered why, exactly, she was so buzzed right now. Was it simply the rush of making a new friend? Or was it a crush? Did she feel like this simply because Isabella was so impressive and for some reason wanted to talk to *her*?

She moved away from the glass as if it had burnt her. What if she started prattling on one night, and Isabella realized how boring and dumb she was? She took a deep breath and focused her gaze on a piece of paper blowing down the sidewalk in the windy night. It looked like a flyer, and Erin forced her brain to try and focus on what color it was. She had to distract herself—ground herself—from these worries, or she'd be up all night freaking out. The flyer looked red and green, but then it blew out of her line of sight.

Erin pondered having more coffee but knew that it would only fizz her brain up and get her heart pounding even more. Why was her heart pounding? *This is ridiculous.*

She stopped her racing brain. Maybe she was just sexually frustrated? Maybe this was, at least in part, physical? She bit her lower lip again, as she considered if that could be it. Was that why her feelings seemed more intense than they should be? She figured it couldn't hurt to try and fix it. If nothing else, a quick orgasm might relax her enough to sleep.

Ten minutes later, Erin had hurried through a hot shower, brushed her teeth, and gotten under the covers. She let her hands find their way between her legs, and her mind conjured the images she needed to get her to a state of arousal and then to climax. It was perfunctory, more like massaging aching shoulders than making love to herself.

She had been told by former lovers that this wasn't how they touched themselves. Hell, Katie said she lit scented candles and put on romantic music. But for Erin, it was just a physical need taken care of. It was the touch and care from another person that made the act of reaching an orgasm fun or meaningful. And she couldn't have that now. All she could hope for tonight was to feel relaxed and content, physically if not mentally. She felt the last shudder of her orgasm, and slowly brought her hands back to her sides. Her body softened, and while her breathing calmed to normal, and her brain was quiet in blissful relaxation.

It lasted all of a minute, before a stray thought popped into her head. *I wonder if Isabella ever touches herself?*

Erin slapped her hand over her face. Her brain backed off in shame and provided a more platonic option. *Where does Isabella sleep? It's clearly with Alberto but away from Richard. Does she have a bed in Alberto's room? Has she told me this and I forgot?*

"Stop thinking about her!" Erin shouted at herself in frustration. "You're supposed to be sleeping, dumbass!"

She regretted shouting a second later, when she heard an angry banging from her neighbor in the apartment next to hers.

"Sorry!" She shouted toward the wall, hoping they didn't think she was just responding with more noise.

It was getting late, but she was clearly not close to sleep. She groaned and turned on the TV. Hopefully, there would some truly dull infomercial that would make her fall asleep. She got as comfortable as she could and tried to focus on being sold face-care products which apparently would have the same effect as surgery, the fountain of youth, and bathing in virgin's blood.

The infomercial trick hadn't worked. In the end, pure fatigue and the muted sounds of the city that never sleeps sent Erin to sleep at 5 a.m.

Since Erika wasn't coming over until one thirty, Erin went back to bed after a rushed breakfast of cereal and orange juice. She slept fitfully, waking every time there was a noise outside, and gave up at ten fifteen. She did some crunches and squats, had a long shower, and ate peanut butter on whole grain bread for an early lunch.

She picked up her phone and checked the time. 12:38 p.m. She grunted in frustration. God, the day was dragging.

She was nervous about seeing Erika; she'd been terrible at keeping in touch. Annoyingly, she was intensely restless too. She didn't want to think about that, because she knew her restlessness was because of Isabella, or to be precise, her feelings for Isabella.

Erin took a chance, opened her phone's contact list, found Erika, and tapped the *call* button. She flexed her biceps and licked her lips, those tics she did when she was nervous.

"Hey, sweetie. Everything okay? Not calling to cancel, I hope?" Erika joked.

Erin smiled. Erika's voice sounded like she always did, smart and considerate, a calming tonic for frayed nerves, which was just what Erin needed right now.

"I'm good. And no, not canceling. In fact, I was wondering if you were free to meet a little earlier? I can come meet you in Brooklyn, if you're still at home."

"Funnily enough, I'm already on my way to you. Partly because my housemates were driving me crazy, and partly because I wanted to stop by that tiny Italian bakery and buy some of those cannoli you like as a surprise."

Erin chewed the inside of her cheek. "Okay, um. I'll meet you down there, then? Is that okay?"

"Of course it is. Are you sure you're all right? It's not like you to be this impatient. I mean, I'm glad you've missed me and all, but it's still a bit unusual for you."

"Yeah, I just need to talk. I'll see you at the bakery soon." Erin reached for her jacket.

"Okay, I'll see you soon, then. Bye."

"Yep," Erin said, the phone wedged between her shoulder and her ear. She ended the call and shoved the phone into her jeans pocket.

She fastened the zipper to her lumberjack-style leather jacket. It had a hood, was lined with thick, fake fur, and was a little tatty after many a New York winter. It probably needed replacing, but she loved it like a safety blanket. She checked that her keys were in the pocket, then headed for the elevator.

Riding the damn thing down seemed to drag on more than usual, as did the fast-paced walk to the bakery. When she finally arrived, she was out of breath and annoyed. Luckily, her mood changed when she saw her friend.

Erika was at the counter, surveying the pastries and cakes. Her light-colored outfit and platinum-blonde hair made her look like some kind of ice princess. *Very fitting for a Scandinavian,* Erin mused. She just couldn't figure out how Erika kept that outfit from getting covered in city grime in New York. Nevertheless, that was Erika to a tee, almost intimidatingly perfect.

Erin didn't mind. She was one of the few people in their little group of friends who never felt jealous of Erika. She didn't know if it was because she had seen Erika at her lowest, or if jealousy just wasn't a part of her nature. Instead, all she ever felt was the buzz of joy at seeing her friend again. She went over to drape an arm around Erika's shoulder.

"Oh, just order one of each, Swede," Erin said with a grin.

Erika jerked around quickly at the touch but smiled when she saw it was Erin. "You scared me! And I'm not ordering one of each. Not everyone burns off the calories the way you do." She pointed at the case. "What do you want?"

Erin looked down at the treats on display. It was a small bakery, which meant that, through the years she had lived in the neighborhood, she'd sampled all its delights and liked most of them.

"Well, we should get some of the cannoli, like you said. And then a few of those chocolate-dipped biscotti, and a baba ricotta each," Erin replied authoritatively

Erika stared at her. "You know that's enough dessert for a week, yes?"

"Not the way I eat, buddy," Erin said with a shrug.

Erika sighed and turned to the pimpled young guy by the till. She ordered two of each item.

"Only two?" Erin asked with a pout.

"Yes. Only two. I'm not having you eating too much and then starting to do push-ups to try and lose the calories quicker. I had enough of that last time we went out for dinner with Luke."

Erin frowned. "Hey, it wasn't my fault you and Luke were both on a diet. They had a cheesecake sharing platter."

Like a patient mother, Erika smiled at her and then paid the cashier. She walked out with Erin just behind her.

It was one of those sunny but freezing days, and on the way back to her apartment, Erin breathed in deeply and wondered how such polluted city air could still feel so crisp. *That's at least one good thing about winter*, she mused.

Twenty minutes later, they were seated at Erin's little table, which served as both dinner table and desk. The laptop was safely tucked away, and in its usual place were two plates with baked goods and a pot of freshly brewed coffee. Erika poured herself a mug, topping it off with milk, while Erin picked what to eat first. The cannoli won, and she took a big bite just as Erika asked, "So, what is it that you were so eager to talk about?"

She blew on her hot coffee, while Erin swallowed her mouthful much too quickly.

"Well, first of all, I realized I hadn't been seeing my friends as much as I should. I hadn't talked to you or Luke or even Julian in ages. Secondly, I kinda need advice."

Erika took a dainty sip of her coffee. "All right. Regarding your first point, it's not just you. I've been really busy with work and horrible dates, and Luke, well, Luke has met the man of his dreams. Or, at least, so he claims. He and some guy named Shawn are talking about moving in together."

"What? So soon? And people say lesbians move in quickly."

Erika gave a little shrug. "I know. But he says he's sure that Shawn's the one. And after seeing them once in Brooklyn, I'm inclined to agree. They're adorable together and seem well matched. Anyway, what was I going to say? Oh yes, Julian. He is still locked up in his house and refusing to see anyone."

Erin winced but didn't interrupt.

"So, as I was saying," she picked up a biscotti, "it's not just your fault. We've all been busy. When it comes to your second point...well, I'm all ears."

Erin watched her daintily dip the thing in her coffee, wishing that Erika would be a little less perfect in this particular moment. It would be easier to talk about her confused feelings if Erika wasn't so composed and sensible.

That hadn't always been the case, of course. When Erin had first met her in Central Park, Erika had been sitting on a bench crying because her parents had just passed away in an accident. Erin had immediately felt close to the young woman and had held her as she cried. That sort of start made for a sturdy friendship. So, why couldn't Erin just start talking about Isabella now?

Before taking a bite, Erika quietly asked, "Problems of the heart, right?"

Erin stared at her. "Why do you say that?"

"Because if you needed to borrow money or ask me to help you move or something, you would've just said it. Love always messes with your head. And I don't think what happened between you and Katie made things any better. So, just talk to me; it doesn't have to make sense. Just start talking."

Erin took a deep breath and sighed it out. "I met this woman called Isabella online, and we've been chatting a lot. She lives in Florida with her boyfriend and their cute little baby. So, she's obviously taken and just wants a friend, but I can't stop thinking about her twenty-four seven. It would probably be easier to just ignore it if she seemed happy in her relationship, but she never talks about him. She doesn't seem to spend any time with him either."

She looked up at Erika to see if those bright-blue eyes were glaring at her with judgment. She should've known better. Erika just smiled and nodded encouragingly.

"I don't know her all that well, yet. But she's so damn interesting. She's traveled loads, and she's lived a life so totally different from mine, but it was still sorta shitty. She's got this clever and sarcastic front, like a protective wall or something. She gives off this vibe like she doesn't need anyone. But under that, she seems vulnerable and sort of...lost. She's not as messed up as me, though, so I'm sure I couldn't make it work, even if she was single." Erin fidgeted in her seat. "So, yeah. That's my problem. I think I feel something for her. Although she's clearly...you know..."

"Unobtainable?" Erika suggested.

Erin nodded, not at all surprised that a foreigner found the right word before she did. "Yeah, exactly. But I don't know if I have, like, a crush on her, or if it's just that I'm lonely. I mean, we've only talked a few nights, and I'm not really talking to anyone else—outside of work, of course."

Erika's half-eaten biscotti went down on a napkin on the table. "So, you decided to see me to find out if some social interaction would make you think less about her. Snap you out of it, so to speak?"

The thought put a small frown on Erin's face. "Well, I wanted to meet up with you as well. But yeah, I suppose. That and I wanted your advice. What should I do? If I am crushing on this woman, I should stop talking to her, right?"

Erika held up a hand. "I think that would be premature at this point. So far, all you know is that you like talking to her and that you think about her a lot. Correct?"

"Yeah." Even Erin could hear the defeat in her voice.

"Well, maybe it is a crush and will pass when you get to know her better. Perhaps it's just that you are happy to find a new friend and are obsessing about her a little too much, because you're lonely. Or maybe, you've been poisoned by all those protein bars you eat. In conclusion, you need to find out what's going on here."

"I know. But how?" Erin whined before shoving half a biscotti into her mouth.

"There are lots of ways. Look, I honestly think you might be overthinking this a little."

"You mean that I'm freaking out over nothing?"

Erika winced a little. "I wouldn't put it as harshly as that. I just mean you should take it one step at a time and try to relax." She handed Erin a napkin. "Maybe you just need to talk to her a little more in depth. Maybe try a video chat? That is what Skype was designed for, right?" She smiled. "Look, you have to figure out what you're feeling. Everything else can wait until you've done that." She put her hand on Erin's shoulder and gave it a comforting squeeze. "Just talk to the woman." Before Erin had time to reply, Erika spoke again. "Oh, and see how you feel after I've gone. If you are just lonely, surely you'll be thinking about her less after you've had some social interaction. How about I tell you all the gossip about Luke and Shawn, and then we can see what's on at the cinema tonight?"

Erin smiled back and nodded, and hoped Erika was right.

Chapter 12

Pain

SATURDAY EVENING FOUND ISABELLA SITTING in her armchair and feeding Alberto while Richard had gone out for drinks with some coworkers.

Alberto was looking up at her with those pretty, blue-green eyes, and Isabella lost herself in them, marveling at how intelligent they looked for eyes belonging to such a new, helpless little human. He bit a little, and she hissed in pain.

"Ow, careful. You shouldn't be so eager to feed. That is how you give yourself indigestion. Slow down, there's no hurry. It's just you and me tonight. Oh, and maybe a certain woman from New York. What do you think, *cariño*? When you have eaten, should we see if Erin is online?"

His eyes stayed focused on her face, and he reached up a little hand to touch her chin. She encouraged it, knowing that he needed to grow his muscles and his hand-eye coordination in any way possible.

She leaned forward and kissed his tiny fingertips, and her back spasmed painfully.

Annoyingly, Richard was right. Sleeping in this chair was hurting her back. She knew it was bad for her, and she also knew the other mothers in her baby group thought she was spoiling Alberto, being there every time he moved.

That reminded her of the article about babies and physical affection she had promised to e-mail out to the other moms in the group. She should get on with that, not just because she felt they needed to read it, but also because she should make an effort to socialize more. She was no longer getting social interaction at work or from networking parties and business lunches. If she wasn't careful, Erin the self-proclaimed loner, would interact with more people than she did.

As Alberto let go of her breast and lay back in her arms, full and happy, Isabella felt another twinge in her back. She entertained the thought of going back to sleeping in the bedroom, but it just didn't feel right. She didn't feel at home in that bed or, if she was honest with herself, sleeping next to Richard.

"No, I think I'll stay in here with you. I'll just have to find ways to help my back cope."

He gurgled and babbled at her, and she smiled from ear to ear. He'd been a quiet baby when he was born, so she cherished every nonsensical noise he made.

She lifted him to her shoulder to burp him and then walked over to his crib to put him in. She handed him a baby rattle and watched him reach to try and grab it. He finally managed, then dropped the toy just as fast.

"Oops. Not to worry, you'll get there soon. You know, you are at the age where you are supposed to start sleeping through the night, too. What do we think about that? Any chance you'll manage it, or is that silly tummy of yours going to keep you up?"

In response, Alberto smiled and waved his little arms and legs wildly.

Isabella laughed. "Looks like you are as eager as I am to have you sleeping through the night, *mi vida*," she whispered tenderly.

His eyelids were beginning to droop, and she caressed the downy hair on his head and hummed a lullaby until his eyes were fully closed and his breathing was calm.

Isabella stretched, then sat back down in her chair. She picked up her iPad and bit her lip around a smile, as she saw a notification on her Skype app. She opened it and was glad to see that the notification did indeed mean that Erin had messaged her.

> **BlackVelvetBitches:** Hey, Ms. Writer. You online? I am for now, but I'm going to the movies with a friend soon. (Actually she's waiting in the hall and looks grumpy that I'm taking so long. :-D) I just wanted to check if you wanted to chat tonight when I get

back? I want to make sure you haven't freaked out about all my questions about your life last night. ;-) Anyway, gotta go. Hope to see you tonight!

Her wristwatch showed it was only a little after nine. Erin was probably still in the cinema then.

Isabella felt a strange surge of energy pulse through her body. She couldn't imagine anything better. She typed a reply for Erin to see as she left the movie theatre.

IsabellaMartinez1: Of course. I wouldn't abandon my insomnia-and-coffee comrade. Just send me a message when you get back, and hopefully I'll be awake to see it. I hope you and your friend are enjoying the movie.

She wondered what Erin was seeing and who she was with. Hadn't she said that she rarely saw her friends?

Apparently, everyone but she and Alberto were being social tonight. Still, despite her plans, Erin had taken the time to make sure that she could talk to her afterward. The thought made Isabella smile. She put the tablet down and decided to close her eyes for a second. A few breaths later, she was asleep.

She woke with a start. Alberto was crying, and she had no idea what time it was.

She blinked her eyes clear from dried mascara and hurried to get him. She picked him up and walked him around. He still didn't settle. This wasn't a normal waking up, by the sounds of his plaintive crying—his stomach was hurting.

She hated when he was in pain. She couldn't count the amount of times when she had asked the doctors if there was anything she could do, maybe stop eating and drinking something in particular, to help him. But the doctors just kept assuring her that it was normal, nothing to do with her habits, and that he would most likely grow out of it soon.

She did the belly rubbing on his front and then his back, while he lay on the seat of her armchair. After a while, his desperate crying faded to little sobs.

Her own eyes were wet. When he was this upset, she couldn't maintain her steely control. Alberto was her Achilles heel, and when he was in pain, she was in pain. She didn't know if it was physical or mental, but she could feel her breasts ache, the same way they did when she hadn't fed him for a while and they were full. She pushed the sensation away, annoyed at her body's weakness.

She tried to compose herself and cleared her throat. "There, that's better, isn't it, Alberto?"

She dried his wet cheeks with her hand and kissed his little forehead and nose. His hands grabbed hold of fistfuls of her hair, and he clambered close to her, seeking body contact. She held him tight and felt his breathing calm.

Soon he was babbling, his voice a little raspy from crying so loudly. She spoke back in a calming voice, pretending they were having a conversation about his stomach. Obviously, he didn't know what she was saying, but she knew that Alberto hearing speech would help him start to talk sooner and that her voice soothed him.

She'd done so much research when she'd found out she was pregnant. Asking her mother for help had been useless. She had merely stared at Isabella as if she were dumb. She could remember her mother's words clearly.

Isabella, you call yourself independent, and I know you are not an imbecile. Surely you can figure out what a baby needs without books? However, if you want my advice, I recommend getting a full-time nanny and then returning to work. You have money to make and a family name to uphold.

The memory still made her angry. She would not be the cold and distant parent her own mother had been.

Alberto's babbling slowed, and he grew silent and floppy on her shoulder. Even though he was clearly asleep, she didn't dare wake him by putting him into the crib. She sat back down in her chair, Alberto sleeping on her left arm, and her right arm tapping at the iPad perched on her thigh. She checked the time, 11:23 p.m. She opened Skype and saw a message from about ten minutes earlier.

BlackVelvetBitches: Hey! I'm back. I'll be around the laptop, just need to make coffee and stretch my ass and back out after sitting in those shitty chairs in my local movie theatre.

Isabella smirked and wondered exactly how one "stretched their ass." Carefully, so as to not wake Alberto, she replied.

IsabellaMartinez1: Hello there. Sorry to keep you waiting. Me and Alberto actually fell asleep around nine and slept soundly until now. I sympathize with needing to stretch your back. Sleeping in this armchair is wreaking havoc with mine.

The reply from Erin came in right away.

BlackVelvetBitches: That's why we invented beds, I think. Did they not make it down to Florida?

Isabella chuckled wryly, as she rolled her eyes.

IsabellaMartinez1: Haha. Your sense of humor really isn't improving, is it? I have to sleep next to Alberto. You know that.

BlackVelvetBitches: Yeah, I do. Just messing with ya. Well if you want, I can show you some exercises to strengthen your back and stretch it out?

Isabella took a second to think that over. She hated being told what to do, even if it was to help her be more physically comfortable.

IsabellaMartinez1: Yes, as long as you don't nag me about doing the stretches every time we talk.

BlackVelvetBitches: No, ma'am. *salutes*

IsabellaMartinez1: All right, then. Tell me what to do if my lower back feels tense and occasionally spasms.

BlackVelvetBitches: Well, my recommendations to anyone else would be to sleep in a bed and go to regular yoga/Pilates classes. Maybe get a massage once in a while.

Isabella frowned and huffed out a breath, which nearly woke Alberto.

IsabellaMartinez1: I'm losing patience, Miss Black.

BlackVelvetBitches: God, I love it when you call me that! :-D It makes me feel like you're my teacher or something. Okay, I'll be serious. I would recommend three stretches (to start with). 1. child's pose. 2. spinal twist 3. Standing-forward bend.

Isabella's frown deepened.

IsabellaMartinez1: Those all sound terrible. Especially spinal twist, which sounds like some sort of medieval torture.

BlackVelvetBitches: All stretches (especially ones that originate in yoga) have weird-ass names. It's not as bad as it sounds. As you are new to it, you should start with a seated spinal twist.

IsabellaMartinez1: Fine. How do I do it?

BlackVelvetBitches: Well, you sit down cross-legged and with a straight back. Then you place your right foot on the other side of your knee.

Isabella was starting to feel overwhelmed and impatient before they had even begun.

IsabellaMartinez1: I do what? How do you propose I do that without breaking my legs? I'm not very flexible.

BlackVelvetBitches: Okay, we'll do it a simpler way. You'll sit cross-legged, and then put your right hand on floor on the outside of your left hip.

IsabellaMartinez1: And that's supposed to be easier, is it?

BlackVelvetBitches: Sorry, I'm crap at describing what to do. I tend to show my clients how to do the moves while I explain. I'm better with action than words.

Isabella was about to reply, but then there was another message coming in, as if Erin had suddenly thought of something.

BlackVelvetBitches: You know what? What if we do another video call, but this time we both have our cameras on? You can watch me do the stretches and then mimic me. That way, I can see if you are doing them right and give you pointers.

Isabella considered it. It would be the first time she would see Erin on camera, and she had to admit that she was curious. That profile picture with aviator sunglasses didn't show much of Erin, and she knew nothing about what Erin's apartment looked like. Besides, she was getting nowhere with Erin's descriptions, so a demonstration would be helpful. Without it, she was probably going to blow up and show off her short fuse. And she didn't want Erin to see that if it could be helped.

IsabellaMartinez1: That seems like a good idea. Not now, though. Alberto is sleeping, and there's not enough room in here to move without feeling encumbered.

BlackVelvetBitches: Okay, I don't know exactly what that word means, but I get the general idea. What about tomorrow? It's Sunday, so I don't have any clients.

IsabellaMartinez1: That sounds good. Richard is usually away with Joshua (his son from an earlier marriage) on weekends, but this weekend got canceled as Joshua has a cold. So, Richard could take Alberto while you coach me in the art of the child's dragon or whatever it was.

BlackVelvetBitches: It's CHILD'S POSE, woman! :-D Yeah, sure. Tomorrow it is. What time?

Isabella thought through Alberto's schedule. For some reason, she was reticent to book it in too late in the day. She wanted to video chat as soon as possible.

IsabellaMartinez1: Somewhere between Alberto's morning nap and lunch. 11, perhaps?

BlackVelvetBitches: 11 a.m. it is!

IsabellaMartinez1: Agreed. Now, tell me about your day. First off, how was the movie?

BlackVelvetBitches: Not bad. Well, I mean, it was bad. But in the right way, the way action movies are supposed to be bad. Erika wanted to see some artsy movie about a widowed teacher. She tried to sell it to me with the fact that it had lesbians in it, and I was almost swayed. But it's just too much fun to drag her along to silly action movies and watch her raise her eyebrows until they stick to her hairline. :-D

IsabellaMartinez1: Let me get this right, you chose to see a movie that was going to be horrible, just to mess with your friend?

BlackVelvetBitches: Exactly! I'm so glad you get me. Anyway, she knew what I was doing. I've known her for years, and she's well aware of how I do things. She plays along and giggles when she thinks I'm not watching.

IsabellaMartinez1: Seems like a good friendship.

BlackVelvetBitches: It is. She's the kind of friend that you can be away from for months, and when you catch up, it's like you never left.

IsabellaMartinez1: That sounds wonderful. I'm glad you have a friend like that.

BlackVelvetBitches: Yeah, me too. For some reason, I was nervous about seeing her. Probably because I hadn't talked to her for ages and I felt guilty. But the second she started messing with me and smiling at me, I felt like I was coming home. She's great. Always interesting and usually really nice. And smart as a whip. You'd like her.

IsabellaMartinez1: While I don't tend to take to people easily, it does sound like I would like her, yes. If for no other reason than because I trust your taste in people. I've found that introverts tend to choose few people to have in their lives, but choose them well. So, other than the bad movie and the amusing effect it had on your friend, what else happened?

She pulled the blanket over her legs, while Erin replied. Isabella was treated to a very detailed description of the copious amounts of snacks Erika had bought, and which ones Erin had stolen from her. Which seemed to be most of them. This was followed by a complete breakdown of how much exercise she would have to do to burn off those calories.

Isabella smiled and realized that, for some unfathomable reason, she was interested. She could sit there, warm and snug, and "listen" to Erin prattle on about anything and just be...content.

She kept herself from thinking about why she was happy to hear someone so different from herself talking about things that shouldn't interest her and focused on asking follow up questions.

Last night had been all about her, tonight was about Erin. And talking about trivial things, like what seats they both preferred in movie theatres, seemed just...perfect. Stopping for much-needed coffee just after midnight was the icing on the cake.

Even Alberto slept peacefully, allowing his mother to carry on the conversation until 3 a.m., when he woke with a piercing cry.

Isabella excused herself and decided to say good night. With the wailing Alberto in her arms, she struggled to type out a quick message.

> **IsabellaMartinez1:** I better go. We should both try to sleep anyway. Need to be fresh for spinal twists and all that tomorrow. Good night, Erin.

The reply came in right away.

> **BlackVelvetBitches:** Night, Isabella. I hope you and the kid both get some good snoozing done. Sweet dreams, and I'll talk to you tomorrow!

Isabella smiled at the words on the screen, as she rubbed Alberto's back and made soothing, shushing noises. She found herself strangely excited to see Erin the next day, and quickly focused all her energy on suppressing that enthusiasm and on taking care of Alberto.

Chapter 13

Seeing Her Face, at Last

ONCE AGAIN, IT HAD TAKEN Erin ages to get to sleep, but this time she was sure it wasn't her insomnia. It was the excitement and fear of seeing Isabella again.

Of actually seeing Isabella and having Isabella see her as well.

She'd jumped out of bed at 9 a.m., forced down breakfast, and showered. She applied some discreet makeup: foundation, mascara, and a little blush—nothing over the top. She dressed in her Sunday-stay-at-home clothes. Then changed into something dressier for the video chat. Then changed again, before finally settling on a stretchy but figure-hugging flannel shirt and a pair of skinny jeans.

She wanted to look good but not as if she'd made an effort. Then she remembered she was supposed to demonstrate stretches. The skinny jeans had to go. She considered exercise gear but decided there was no point in it for the purpose of just demonstrating a few simple poses.

She tore through her wardrobe for something that was flattering but still stretchy. A pair of dark blue jeggings she'd only worn once fit the bill. She pulled them on and practiced the stretches she planned to show Isabella to check that the jeggings would allow for full movement. It pleased her that looking in the mirror informed her just how good her ass looked in them. It wasn't as perfectly rounded as Isabella's, but it was tight as hell.

She poured a cup of coffee and munched down two carrots while she waited. She mused that her nervous chewing must make her look like Bugs Bunny.

Forcing herself to take deep breaths, she looked down at her chest. She wasn't wearing a bra. She never did on weekends, unless she was going out of course—one of the perks of having small breasts. They didn't need the support system.

Her plaid flannel shirt hid most of the outline of her breasts, but she wondered if the fabric would be thick enough to hide it if her nipples got hard? She swore at herself. It was warm in here, and she was just going to talk to someone and show her some simple exercises. "Chill, you perv," she muttered into her mug of coffee.

Time crept at a snail's pace toward 11 a.m.

Finally, Erin threw herself at the laptop, already booted up and waiting for the last forty-five minutes. She'd also checked the camera and the sound quality on a two-minute video chat with Erika, who was rooting for her and had made Erin promise to let her know how it went.

Erin's stomach felt like it was full of butterflies—drunk, crazy butterflies—all over the place and flying into each other. She felt queasy.

When her laptop blared out the Skype ringtone, she froze, staring at the little square that informed her IsabellaMartinez1 was calling. She swallowed thickly, wiped her sweaty palms on her thighs, and answered. The screen switched to a camera view of a light, sun-drenched room with a woman front and center.

The camera showed Isabella wearing a V-neck, black T-shirt, and what looked like the waistband of black yoga pants.

Unlike the time Erin had accidentally seen her, today she was fully made-up. Her glowing skin looked perfectly even, and her eyes were rimmed, giving her a sultry— almost dangerous—look. Her plump lips gleamed in a way that made Erin think she was wearing tinted lip gloss.

Erin wondered if she should've gone with her first choice of dressier clothes. She shook it off. Maybe Isabella was going out with her son and boyfriend afterward, and that was the reason she looked so great.

"Good morning," Isabella said with a tentative smile.

That voice. That freaking, mesmerizing voice. Erin hit her thigh with her fist to make herself reply and not just sit there staring like an idiot.

"H-Hi...um...how are you?" Erin hit herself again for stammering.

"I'm fine, thank you. How are you? Did you manage to get some sleep?"

"I'm good too. Not a lot, no. Making up for it with extra coffee." Erin held up her mug as evidence.

Isabella smiled, and Erin felt her breath catch. The smile faded quickly, and Erin desperately wished it would come back.

"I'm glad I'm not the only one who failed on the sleep front," Isabella said darkly.

"Sorry to hear that. Was it the lil' man who kept you up?"

Isabella opened her mouth to say something, then seemed to think better of it and simply replied, "Yes."

Erin's brain was working overtime. Was Isabella about to say something else? Was something wrong? Had she not slept because she had fought with her boyfriend? Or maybe she had been dreading this chat. Maybe she really didn't want to do these stretches?

Isabella tucked her hair behind her ears and cleared her throat. "Anyway, should we get the exercises over and done with? I'm not really comfortable wearing my running pants indoors."

Is she going to just take them off when we're done stretching? With effort, Erin forced the ridiculous thought away, stood up, and said, "Sure, hang on a sec."

She moved her chair, pushed the table further away from the wall, and tilted the laptop screen, with its camera, to face down so that Isabella could see her whole body. She wondered why she hadn't done this before the call started. And why she hadn't given up on her vanity and just worn her damn exercise gear.

She'd been so excited to see Isabella that she hadn't thought this part through. *Well, that's one point in the I-have-a-crush column.*

She looked at the screen. Isabella was standing up too. Her black trousers were a tight, Lycra-like material with reflective stripes on the sides, clearly running pants.

Erin was about to ask Isabella if she wanted to go out running together one day, then cursed her own stupidity. *Different states, Erin. Idiot!*

She could also see that Isabella was surrounded by a large expanse of wooden floor for her to use and still stay on camera. Unlike her, Isabella had clearly prepped properly for the exercises. The floor was nice and looked expensive. However, it looked hard, and that made Erin realize she had forgotten something else.

"Oh, man. I'm sorry. I forgot to ask you to get a blanket or a thick towel or something to put on the floor. Can you go get something real quick?"

Isabella looked around. "There is a thick rug behind me. I can pull that over here?"

"Yeah, that'll probably do it. Just anything to make you comfy on the floor. Maybe invest in a cheap yoga mat or something if you're going to do this a lot."

"Yes, that's a good idea." Isabella said. She walked out of view, probably to drag the rug over to the computer.

Erin fetched her threadbare yoga mat and rolled it out. She looked at the screen and saw a plush, burgundy rug under Isabella's feet.

"Great. Now, can you get on it so I can make sure the camera angle is right?"

Isabella sat down cross-legged on the mat and gave her a brief smile. Heat filled Erin's chest and stomach. Isabella fluctuated between looking jaded and completely in control, to that tentative and unsure smile in seconds. It did strange things to Erin's insides.

"Right. So, let's start with child's pose. It's a yoga move, and I think it'll be good to start with. It's gentle and a really nice stretch for your back." She knelt down. "Can you still see me all right?"

"Yes, I can see you," Isabella said and got down on her knees too.

"Great. Okay, you'll want to sit down with your, um, buttocks on your feet. Then spread your knees wide while keeping your toes touching." Erin demonstrated, then watched Isabella mirror her movements. It was unnerving, having Isabella look at her so closely. It shouldn't have been. Clients watched her every day to see how to do their exercises. But this was different. She tried to breathe slowly and ignore the goose bumps forming on her arms.

"Perfect. Then you bow forward so that your torso is lying between your knees and your forehead is on the floor. When you get to that point, you can choose to either have your arms stretched out in front of you—which I prefer, because I find it stretches my shoulders nicely—or you can have your arms lying by your sides, resting comfortably with your palms up."

"I'll stick with whatever is most efficient."

Erin wasn't sure that efficiency was the point of this pose, more relaxation and stretching. But the last thing she wanted was to overcomplicate things and make Isabella dislike the routine.

"Whatever works for you, I'll be stretching my arms out. Okay, so watch me and ask questions if you need to."

Erin laid her torso down and stretched her arms out. When Erin had practiced the stretches in her jeggings before, she hadn't done this pose. She wished she had. The jeggings were fine, but the shirt was riding up her back, exposing far more skin to the camera then she would've liked. She started to feel self-conscious again.

"You look like you are praying to that lamp," Isabella said in a sarcastic tone.

Erin gave a snorting laugh while staying in the pose. She knew what Isabella meant. The pose did make people look like they were worshipping whatever was in front of them. Erin had decided to do the pose sideways, so Isabella could see more of her body, and she was facing a hideous floor lamp that she'd bought in a secondhand shop a year ago.

"Just copy the position, snarkypants," Erin said, her voice muffled by the pose.

"Very well," Isabella muttered.

Erin counted to five very slowly and then looked up. Isabella was doubled over with her arms out in front of her. She was doing the move sideways too, and Erin got a view of her entire body.

She was very happy that her brain focused on two quite innocent features, the mass of shiny black hair pooling around Isabella's head on the floor and her bare feet, tucked under her rear with only the toes sticking out.

Still, the luscious mass of hair made Erin feel like she was observing a goddess or something, while the cute little toes reminded her that it was a woman of flesh and blood she was staring at. She was smiling like an idiot and was damn grateful that Isabella couldn't see it.

"Good. Now take deep breaths from your belly and try to feel your lower back expanding," Erin said.

She could see Isabella was doing as she was asked. The slightly arched back lifted a little with every deep breath and then sank onto her thighs as she exhaled.

Erin's hands tingled with the desire to put her hands on Isabella's back and softly caress her form. Strangely, she felt so full of emotion, so filled to the brim with tenderness and excitement when she looked at Isabella, that there could be no doubt as to what she was feeling.

Her smile turned melancholy. Unrequited crushes were always devastating; she'd been there plenty of times before.

Now wasn't the time. She needed to focus on the stretches, on Isabella. She pulled on her professionalism and showed Isabella each move she'd suggested. She had her do each one for ten slow breaths, then start over from the top.

Although she made grouchy comments throughout, Isabella was quick to learn and seemed dedicated to performing the stretches correctly. Erin was impressed.

When they'd finished, Erin stood up and glanced at her wrist, only to swear quietly to herself.

"What's the cursing about?" Isabella asked, as she stood up and smoothed her hair.

"Sorry, I didn't mean to say that out loud. I just keep looking at my wrist for the time, but I broke my watch a few days ago."

Looking back at the screen, she noticed Isabella staring at her naked arm. Her goose bumps returned.

"Well, that's a nuisance. I'd be really annoyed if I didn't have my watch." Isabella pointedly looked away from Erin's arm.

"Um, yeah. It's annoying. I'll probably buy a new one with my next paycheck."

Erin slowly adjusted her ponytail. She didn't want the call to end, but she wasn't sure she should continue it either. She decided to leave it up to Isabella, hoping she would know what was best for them both.

Chapter 14

Isabella Takes a Deep Breath (Or Is It Ten?)

ISABELLA WAS ANNOYED. HER BREATHING was rapid, and she struggled to pull her gaze away from her PC.

On the screen she usually used only for her writing, was a blonde, athletic woman in jeggings and a flannel shirt. Erin looked relaxed, casual—a fit woman doing stretches as easy for her as walking to the car.

Unlike her, in exercise gear, whose unused muscles thrummed after the stretches. She'd probably overdone it, simply because she wanted to seem in shape in front of Erin. Why hadn't she asked Erin what she should wear? She was angry, because she felt foolish, but that wasn't the only reason she was annoyed.

No. She was annoyed, because she couldn't stop staring at the extraordinarily beautiful blonde on the screen. Erin had high cheekbones, a little dimple in her chin, and the most infectious smile Isabella had ever seen. To make it worse, she also had amazing eyes that flashed more green than blue in the pale New York sunlight. Erin Black was effortlessly stunning, and Isabella found it hard to look away.

Isabella found her clean, fresh beauty a little intimidating. She tried so hard with makeup and expensive clothes to feel her best—to look her best. Still, she doubted she could ever be truly intimidated by Erin. Her personality made it impossible. She was too lovable, too down to earth.

It was annoying. Erin's beauty was annoying. Her awkwardness and those confusingly evocative glances were annoying. But most annoying of all was her own absolute attraction to Erin. She shouldn't feel this. And she hated how out of control she felt.

Erin was standing up, her hands wedged into the tight pockets at her hips. "So, um, do you want to try anything else or...?"

Isabella knew she should end the call. Just end it, get changed out of her ridiculous clothes, and go check on Alberto and Richard. But she didn't want to. She wanted to keep looking at Erin. She wanted to ask Erin to smile for her again. *Despicable! You're in a relationship.* She shouldn't be mooning over another woman. How had she become so...pathetic...so fast?

She took a deep breath. It didn't help.

"No, I should probably go. Richard can't be left alone with Alberto. The clumsy idiot would probably drop him." It had been meant as a joke, but due to her annoyance with herself, it came out as an insult.

The woman on the screen took a step back and frowned.

"Geez, Isabella. That's kinda unfair, isn't it? I thought you said Richard was a good dad?"

Isabella felt her skin grow hot. She was overloaded with emotion. Embarrassed, angry, and painfully confused by what she was feeling.

"How would you know? You know nothing about him or me, Erin. Don't you dare judge me for what I say about the man I live with."

"Hey, relax. I was just pointing out that you were being a bit harsh. I don't know the guy at all, but you've told me he's great with both his kids, so I kinda have to go on that." Erin looked like she was about to stop but then carried on talking. "Oh, and I do know quite a bit about you, actually. I may not be your bff or anything, but don't pretend I'm not getting to know you pretty well here."

Isabella was about to give a biting reply. She could shut this little discussion down with speed and merciless efficiency, no matter how upset she was. She could win this.

But she looked into those beautiful, blue-green eyes and that firm, stubborn gaze and she didn't want to. Erin stood so tall and proud, her beautiful features locked in a frown. Her eyes were a similar color to her beloved Alberto's. This was clearly one of those times when Erin stood up for what was right, like she'd mentioned when they first met, the savior of all who needed someone to stand up for them.

Isabella shouldn't fight that. She wouldn't. Especially not when she knew that her horrible temper was to blame here. *She* was to blame here. Her anger dissolved, like ice on a hot plate.

"You're right. That sounded harsher than I meant. I'm not in the best of moods today. I apologize for being so brusque. I'll make it up to Richard with his favorite lunch later. And you're right, you are getting to know me. Very well, actually. Anyway, I," she paused, "should still go check on Alberto and Richard."

"That's all right. We all have our off days." Erin's voice immediately lost its edge. She squinted and added, "Hang on, I just need to pull this blind. The sun's in my eyes."

While Erin adjusted her blind to shut out the winter sun, Isabella took a breath. She'd found another big difference between Richard and Erin: Richard always pulled back when her temper flared and she'd been unfair. Afterward, he would avoid her for days, sulking without letting her explain or apologize.

Erin, on the other hand, said her piece. And when the issue was resolved, she apparently let it go and carried on as normal. Was she always like that, or just in this situation?

Isabella shook her head and berated herself for comparing her new friend to her boyfriend. It wasn't fair. Her stomach ached with a knot of self-loathing. She sat up, trying to make the feeling go away. She just wasn't thinking straight today. She was too preoccupied with a messy ponytail of gleaming blonde hair and a smile that hit her like a rush of hot air on a freezing day. Why did Erin have to be so attractive on top of being so charming and interesting? It really wasn't fair.

Erin scratched the back of her neck. "So I guess we should hang up so you can go check on your boys and make lunch?"

"Yes, I'm afraid so. What are you going to do?"

"Actually, lunch sounds like a good idea. After that, who knows?"

"Meet up for midnight coffee again?" Isabella asked with a smile she hoped was charming.

"Sure! Well, it's usually a bit before midnight, isn't it? I've got no big plans, other than seeing you that is."

"Me neither. So me and a sleeping Alberto will chat with you tonight?"

Erin nodded, smilingly. "It's a date. Well, I mean, it's not a *date* date. It's just, you know, a saying."

Isabella laughed and held up a hand to stop her. "I get it, Miss Black. I look forward to talking to you tonight. Bye for now."

Erin waved goodbye and then bent over to the laptop, presumably to end the call.

Isabella growled angrily at the universe, as Erin's shirt fell open and revealed a smooth expanse of skin building to two mounds.

Isabella didn't have time to see much, but she looked close enough to know there was no bra under that shirt. It was just as intriguing as Erin's shirt riding up her back when she had demonstrated child's pose, exposing her slim waist and exquisitely sculpted back muscles. *Does she have abs that sculpted too?* Isabella shivered at the prospect.

She shouldn't be thinking like this. She clenched her fists by her sides and took slow, calming steps toward the bedroom where Richard was playing with Alberto.

She gently opened the door and saw Richard bent over their child, blowing a raspberry on his naked belly.

"Oh hey, Isabella. Junior here is in his birthday suit because he decided to throw up all over his outfit. Where are his clean clothes?"

Isabella went to Alberto and looked at him with concern. He seemed all right, happy and playful and instantly babbling when he saw his mother.

"He vomited? Without having eaten?"

Richard shrugged. "Yeah, I think I might have tossed him around a little too much. I don't know. He looks okay again now."

Isabella took a breath to calm herself. It seemed to be all she was doing today. "Yes, probably just his stomach playing up in combination with the effects of the roughhousing. He seems fine now," she agreed.

"He's all right, Isabella. Babies throw up sometimes. He's not made of glass. I don't get why you worry so much."

She gave a weak smile at his words and held her tongue. How could she not worry? Alberto was her everything. And right now, he was the only thing keeping her from being torn apart by doubts about her relationship and strange feelings for a certain personal trainer.

An hour later, her father called to ask how she and Alberto were doing. Isabella gave a brief rundown—all safe, uncontroversial small talk. When she mentioned how much hair Alberto had now, her father immediately asked for a Skype call so he could see for himself.

And here she was, holding up her baby in front of the computer's camera.

Alberto Sr. cooed at his little namesake, but Isabella couldn't see his expression. He claimed his computer's camera was broken, but Isabella suspected he just hadn't set it up correctly. If she was bad with technology, her father was just plain awful with it.

Her father, still speaking in Spanish, as they had since the conversation started, admired the tufts of black hair and pointed out how big Alberto had become. Isabella was just about to reply, when she heard her mother's voice somewhere in the background.

"Switch to English, Alberto. I might want to be part of this conversation when I have gotten rid of this overpaid imbecile. If that ever happens. I'm starting to despair."

Alberto dutifully switched to English.

"I don't know if you heard that. It was your mother."

Isabella placed her son in her lap and fussed with him, looking away from the camera to hide her frustration. "Yes, I heard the royal decree. English it is. Sounds like she's more annoyed than usual."

He sighed. "Yes. My poor, overworked heroine. She's pacing the house, on hold with her new assistant back in the office. There is some sort of emergency regarding a new client. If she grips that phone any harder, I think it might crack."

He whispered those last words, as always, scared to cause offense to his beloved, yet feared, wife. Isabella changed the topic while she still could. No doubt her mother would bring the limelight back to herself any moment.

"How are you, Daddy?"

"I'm very well, thank you. Missing my children, of course. Marie hasn't been to visit for a while. She seems very busy with work."

"Yes, I'm sure she is," Isabella muttered.

If her father had picked up on the tone, he was ignoring it. As always.

"Still, at least she doesn't work as hard as you did. You practically lived in your office."

Isabella grabbed on to Alberto's little hand, which was reaching for the computer mouse. "Yes, I suppose I did."

"Quite the difference to how you're living now, *mija*. Do you miss it?"

"Sometimes. I miss the social interaction. And I miss the fast pace. I have far too much time to think about things now."

She regretted the admission the second the words left her mouth. What was wrong with her lately? She was opening up at the strangest times. She loved her father and missed him, but she was well aware that every word and look on her face would be reported back to her mother. And Judith Martinez would use every scrap of information to meddle in her life. Again. Before her father could ask something about the "too much time to think" comment, Isabella latched on to something her father had mentioned at the start of the call.

"You mentioned a present?"

She heard her father clapping his hands together and wished she could see him. She knew he only did that when he was very excited about something. Isabella could imagine his beaming smile and the twinkle in his big brown eyes. She ached with how much she missed him. She would have done anything to hug him right now.

"Ah, yes," he exclaimed. "I've found an early edition of *Peter Pan* for little Beto. Almost mint condition and beautiful binding."

Isabella's heart warmed, and she tried not to sound patronizing.

"Daddy, it's a little early for that. You might want to start with a picture book. We'll save J.M. Barrie for another five or ten years."

He laughed. "Well, it will probably be five or ten years until we next see you."

Isabella struggled to keep her facial expression neutral. She knew that her mother wanted her to simply bundle up the baby, drop everything, and travel to Philadelphia on a weekly basis. In fact, now that she thought about it, Isabella wasn't sure if her mother wouldn't prefer if she left Alberto with a nanny and visited by herself. She could explain how that wasn't going to work until she was blue in the face. Her mother wouldn't listen, while her father would just look miserable, because he understood but still missed her and his grandson.

The few times she had convinced her parents to travel to Florida had been filled with complaints and snide remarks from her mother and those endless pained smiles and uncomfortable silences from her father. He seemed to almost blend into the wallpaper when his wife and daughter would fight over whatever remark Judith had just made.

"Hopefully, it won't be that long." It was all that Isabella could think to say. She could hear her mother talking on the phone in the background and had no doubt that Judith was keeping one ear on their conversation.

"No. Hopefully not." Her father's voice sounded quiet. Hurt. "Still, at least we do see you now. I know I talk about this a lot, but it was horrible during the period where we had no contact."

She had to agree. Those first few months in Florida, when she had cut ties with her mother, had been hard. Not being able to speak to her father had been frustrating and heartbreaking and the ultimate reason for her reinstating contact again. She knew, now, that taking a stand against her mother and cutting her out of her life would mean the loss of contact with her father, her childhood hero and greatest comfort. It was a thought Isabella didn't want to contemplate and wouldn't be something she'd easily do again. Though she was realistic enough to admit that the need to be free of Judith and her meddling might make it increasingly tempting, wrenching Daddy out of Isabella's life was her mother's greatest trump card.

For the millionth time, Isabella wished that her father was stronger—not so dependent on her mother, not so awed and cowed by his wife. She would never know what he saw in her. Was there something in him that needed her dominance? Her strict rules?

She smiled at the camera. "I know what you mean. I missed you terribly. I missed our phone calls and our letters."

"What you missed were my book recommendations. Admit it, *mi vida*," he said playfully.

She laughed. "Well, yes, that is something I did miss. I read a lot of trash because I didn't have your quality control on tap. And I missed your cooking too. In fact, I still do. When was the last time you made me *asopao*?"

"Far too long. I haven't made it since you left. There is only me who eats it, so I don't see much point. In fact, I don't cook much anymore. Only breakfast, because it is my favorite. Judith often eats at the club for lunch and dinner, unless she skips eating all together or has to attend work functions. You know how it is, schmoozing the clients over dinner. So, I just fix myself up something quick or eat at Santiago's. He has hired a great cook, whom I like to exchange recipes with."

Isabella tried not to frown. Cooking was one of her father's passions. It saddened her that something so important had been taken from him. That he would allow it to be taken from him. She wished he could understand that he deserved better.

She paused at that thought. It was so easy to make those judgments from the outside looking in. It wasn't so easy when you were at the center of those decisions, was it? Daring to think that you deserved better? Daring to ask for what you want. Or, worse still, recognizing the things you need for something as frivolous as personal happiness.

Isabella listened to her father talk about Santiago's chef and the recipes he had introduced him to. But her mind was consumed with thoughts of allowing oneself to be happy. Was it truly so selfish to think you deserved to be happy?

Chapter 15

Erin Black's Aching Heart

ERIN PICKED UP HER PHONE and wrote a succinct text to Erika.

Yep, I've got a crush. I'm so screwed.

The reply came back after a few minutes.

I'm sorry, sweetie. So, you're sure now?

Yeah. I mean, I think so. Can I have feelings for someone I have only talked to online? That's a thing, right?

Of course it is a thing. Can I call you to talk about this instead of texting?

Erin rubbed her forehead.

'Kay. I guess.

The phone rang, and when Erin answered, she heard Erika's gentle voice.

"Hey, sweetheart. Yeah, of course it's a thing. Do you remember that I told you about my sister, Annika, back in Sweden?"

Erin thought for a second. "Uh, yeah. I think so."

"Well, she is married to a guy called Kristoffer. He's of Sami descent, which is really cool, but I digress. Anyway, because he's from the north and she's from the south, they met online, on a forum for their favorite book series."

"What books?" Erin asked, knowing full well how Erika would roll her eyes at the interruption. Erin would take her little pick-me-ups where she could get them right now. Annoying Erika a little fit the bill.

"*A Song of Ice and Fire*, but that doesn't matter. Annika says that they didn't even exchange pics until after she'd fallen for him. They've been married for three years and are so in love and so perfectly matched. She says she prefers how it happened between them. Having a long-distance relationship meant they *really* had to get to know each other."

Erin frowned, wondering if she was too tired and upset for a conversation. "How do you mean?"

"Say that you or I date someone in the city, we would probably go out with them, right? We'd go do something like ice skating or see a movie or bowling. Or even just getting drunk in a bar and dancing."

"Yeah, I suppose."

"Well, online, all they could really do was talk. So they got to know each other very well before they even met to start doing stuff like bowling or ice skating. Just talking can make for a very intense and intimate start to a relationship. It speeds up the process because of all the instant sharing."

"Yeah, well, it would only be a start of a relationship if we were both single and into chicks," Erin said dejectedly.

"Ah, yes. Sorry. I was just trying to make sure you didn't doubt your feelings. You can fall for someone online after quite a short time. From what you said yesterday, she is attracted to women, or at least open to it. The only thing standing in your way is the boyfriend, and pardon me for pointing this out, but you said she seemed pretty unhappy with him."

"Sure, but I'm not going to hang around and hope she breaks up with her boyfriend. Anyway, she lives all the way down in goddamned Florida. And she has a big house and a baby. She's so...organized and adult, and me... Well, I'm just me."

"Not so just. You're wonderful. Anyway, it could still work."

"Erika, come on," Erin said tiredly.

"What? It could. Look, what I think you have to decide is if you want to keep being friends and hope your crush passes, or if you need to stop talking to her because you're falling in love with her."

Erin squeezed her eyes closed and felt her free hand ball into a fist. "I...I don't know. Not yet. I, um, I think I'm gonna vacuum the apartment,

I do my best thinking while doing cardio, and this will have the added benefit of getting rid of the dust bunnies."

"Okay. Just text me if you need to talk. Don't bottle it all up," Erika said softly.

"Yeah, I will. Thanks."

"Anytime. Oh, and by the way, I'm glad we are back in touch, Erin. Meet up again soon?"

"I'd like that."

She smiled for the first time since she hung up with Isabella.

About five minutes later, *Wicked Ones* by Dorothy was blasting through her laptop's speakers, and Erin had to force herself to focus on plugging her vacuum cleaner instead of dancing. She started chasing dust bunnies and was glad to see the floor getting cleaner but disappointed to notice that her melancholy was only slightly relieved.

She couldn't stop thinking about Isabella and how amazing it could be if they were together. She couldn't stop wondering if Isabella listened to music while she vacuumed and couldn't stop daydreaming about cleaning and dancing to music with Isabella in a house the two of them lived in. She cursed herself. *Dammit! Would you stop craving things that aren't yours to crave, Black?*

Suddenly, a ballad came on. She rolled her eyes at herself; she must have set it to shuffle her playlists, because there were no slow songs on the cleaning playlist, that was for damn sure.

Still, she didn't switch back to the original playlist. She was too preoccupied with her thoughts about Isabella to care about anything else.

The song ended and another started, just as Erin switched off the vacuum, glad she was done. Another slow song filled the room. Another song that would do nothing to improve her mood. *The Last Beat of My Heart*, by Siouxsie and the Banshees.

Great, a sad song about loving someone even though it's going to hurt like hell. Subtle, universe. Very subtle. Thanks.

Erin sighed and went over to the laptop, intent on skipping to a more cheerful song, but she stopped her fingers just before reaching touchpad. Those lyrics were so damn beautiful. The song was crying out to be danced to, dancing close, holding the person you loved with every beat of your heart. Isabella couldn't be that person, though. Not for Erin. She knew that. Didn't she know that?

She listened to the words, over and over, that were asking—begging—a loved one not to walk away, promising to love them until the very last beat of your heart. And every word, every emotion, every painful, pitiful, beautiful thought seemed to be taken directly from her own head. Or maybe it was from her heart. Either way…it hurt like hell.

The refrain cut her to the core. How on earth could she wish for this? How could she put herself through loving someone who couldn't love her back?

Slowly, grudgingly, the question morphed in her mind. How could she ask for something… *someone*…who wasn't hers to ask for.

It was just like her to ask—want, need, wish—for more than she could have. She remembered one of the bigger kids in her first group home, Jason, accusing her of being spoiled and selfish, because she always wanted the toy someone else had. Maybe this was a pattern with her, wanting what she couldn't have? Or maybe she just had a talent for making herself miserable.

She sat down on her bed and looked at the abandoned vacuum cleaner. The song faded out, but the melancholy words hung in the air.

What was she going to do? Suffer in silence and hope it went away? Or did she dare to be open with Isabella? No, that was probably a dumb idea. Making a decision when she was this emotional… Now that was, without question, a dumb idea. Suddenly, everything felt very bleak.

Erin collapsed back onto the bed. The tears in her eyes made the ceiling look blurry. She hated being this emotional and whiny, but she just felt so goddamned alone. She considered calling Erika again but felt like she would be bothering her. She was a grown woman; she should be able to handle an unrequited crush—and a sad song that brought up every single one of her insecurities—without blubbing to her friend like a baby.

This was pointless. She couldn't just lie here, crying in bed. She forced herself to move and clean up as best she could with cold water and then some makeup to try and look human again. She drank down a cup of coffee while it was still too hot for her throat. Once her gym gear was ready, she headed out. A hard workout was the only thing that could help her now.

It was a little past ten, and the exercise had worked its usual calming magic.

She decided to switch on the laptop and look for Isabella. She still felt shaken up and melancholy, but at least her head felt a little clearer. She still didn't know what to do, but she figured she'd give it a day or two before she made up her mind.

Isabella was already online, and Erin's heartbeat quickened. She pictured the dimly lit room she'd seen when Isabella had shown her Alberto. She visualized the armchair that Isabella slept in, how she must cuddle up to get a few hours of sleep while listening to her son breathing. Suddenly, she desperately wanted—needed—to see Isabella, so much so that it stung.

She shook her head and typed a message, trying for a casual and playful tone.

> **BlackVelvetBitches:** Hey there, Stretchy! How's your back feeling?

> **IsabellaMartinez1:** Like it's been through the wringer, but a little less tense already. I'll certainly keep doing those stretches. Thank you so much for demonstrating.

> **BlackVelvetBitches:** Glad to help! You can return the favor. Next time I need my resume updated, I'll send it to you, Ms. Writer. :-)

It took a while before Isabella replied, and Erin wondered if Alberto had woken up. She took a sip of her coffee and bit into her apple-pie-flavored protein bar.

> **IsabellaMartinez1:** I can do better than that. If you tell me your address, I'll split my bag of Azúcar Negra coffee in two and send you one in the mail.

> **BlackVelvetBitches:** Whoa! Really? Isn't that stuff like a million bucks for two coffee grounds?

> **IsabellaMartinez1:** No, it is not. Do you want the coffee or not?

Erin chuckled. She could hear Isabella's dark tone in the typed words. She wrote out her address and ended with a smiley face icon.

IsabellaMartinez1: Got it. Thank you.

BlackVelvetBitches: No, thank you for the coffee fix!

IsabellaMartinez1: It's the least I could do in exchange for your help and as an apology for my outburst about Richard.

That last message was posted with lightning speed, and Erin wondered if Isabella had thought out what she wanted to say in advance.

BlackVelvetBitches: Hey, I'm not the person you should apologize to. :)

IsabellaMartinez1: No, I suppose not. Still, I want you to know I don't think those things about him. It was just misplaced anger. He and I aren't in the best of places with our relationship, but he is a good man.

Erin knitted her brow. How the hell was she supposed to reply to that?

BlackVelvetBitches: No, you don't seem all that in love with him. (Hope you don't mind me being honest here.)

Was that out of line? Suddenly Erin's palms felt sweaty.

IsabellaMartinez1: No, I don't mind, and trust me when I say that's rare for me. Me and Richard, it's complicated. I actually wrote it all down and described it not that long ago. Funnily enough, I seemed to address it to you.

BlackVelvetBitches: But you never sent it to me?

There was a pause. Erin reached for her protein bar, but she'd lost her appetite. She wrapped it back up and put it on the table.

IsabellaMartinez1: No. It felt too intimate. I didn't know you very well then.

BlackVelvetBitches: And now?

Another pause. Erin wondered if it was warm in the room, or if it was just her.

IsabellaMartinez1: Maybe I'll print it and send it with your coffee?

BlackVelvetBitches: I'd like that. I like learning stuff about you.

IsabellaMartinez1: Sorry, Alberto's waking up.

Erin nodded at the screen, even though Isabella couldn't see her. She blew out a breath, leaned back in her chair, and put her hands behind her neck. She didn't know what she should do, and talking to Isabella only made her more confused.

A few minutes later, there was a message from Isabella.

IsabellaMartinez1: I'm back. Shall we talk about something a little lighter than my relationship problems?

Erin searched for topics to talk about but came up short. All she wanted was to see Isabella's face. She sat up straighter. That was it—Isabella's face…

BlackVelvetBitches: You know, you never answered me about the scar. You know, the one I saw when you accidentally turned the camera on, and I freaked you out? How did you get it? It's really cool, so I'm expecting you to say that you tried to kiss a mountain lion or something.

IsabellaMartinez1: Well, I seem to recall asking you once how much (or how little) you sleep each night, and then we were interrupted. Answer my question, and I'll answer yours.

Erin chuckled. This woman certainly kept her on her toes.

BlackVelvetBitches: Hey, no fair. I asked first…

IsabellaMartinez1: Fine. But you have to promise not to laugh.

BlackVelvetBitches: I'll try. (Not that you'll hear it if I do.)

IsabellaMartinez1: All right. Brace yourself, because this is going to get long. I got the scar dueling with my sister Marie. Well, she wasn't my foster sister at that point. We were babysitting her. I think I told you about Marie but not how she came to live with us. I'll explain about that another time. Anyway, I was six and she was three. She kept nagging me to pretend to be dueling with swords. I wanted her to stop bothering me, and thought I'd scare her a little. So, reckless child that I was, I got two pairs of scissors from the kitchen to duel with. I thought she'd see them and run off crying. Sadly for me, she wasn't scared at all, even though her parents had clearly told her she was too young for scissors. She picked them up and started jabbing at me, pretending it was a sword. Long story short, she sliced my lip open. I screamed to high heaven, Daddy took me to the hospital, and they managed to fix most of it. It was deep, though, so they couldn't avoid leaving a scar.

Erin gave a surprised laugh. She wasn't sure what she had expected the story to be, but this wasn't it.

BlackVelvetBitches: You dueled with a toddler? Didn't see that coming.

IsabellaMartinez1: She dueled with me! I expected the little brat to be intimidated and leave me alone. Instead she just shouted, "HAHA," and stabbed me in the face.

Erin laughed so hard that she snorted.

BlackVelvetBitches: That's priceless. :-D

IsabellaMartinez1: You laughed, didn't you?

BlackVelvetBitches: You'll never know, Martinez. ;-) Anyway, I'm glad the cut didn't take an eye out or something.

IsabellaMartinez1: Yes, it could have been much worse. Marie likes to point that out whenever it comes up. Now it's your turn.

Erin sighed as she considered her sleeping habits, estimating the hours in her head. The results were dismal, and it made her feel tired.

> **BlackVelvetBitches:** How much I sleep? It depends. Sometimes it's three or four hours, sometimes I manage a whole night. Sometimes I only get little naps.

> **IsabellaMartinez1:** Do you know why you have insomnia?

> **BlackVelvetBitches:** Nope. My lazy-ass doctor couldn't figure it out either. Not that he tried very hard. He just gave me a prescription for sleeping pills and told me to relax and cut down on the caffeine.

> **IsabellaMartinez1:** And did you?

> **BlackVelvetBitches:** Cut down? Yeah. I stopped completely with caffeine for six months. Worst six months of my life! I actually (weirdly) slept worse. After that, I practically inhaled a pot of coffee and tried every other cure for insomnia I could find online and in library books. Nothing's worked.

Erin saw that Isabella was typing and quickly sent another message to stop her from asking more questions about it. It was bumming her out, and she didn't need that right now. She especially didn't want to dig into the insomnia thing. She had a feeling Isabella wouldn't stop until she knew the cause of it.

"Let's not go there, not tonight," she muttered. She had to change the topic.

> **BlackVelvetBitches:** So, you've got a foster sister, huh? As a former foster kid, I'll give your parents kudos for fostering.

> **IsabellaMartinez1:** Well, it wasn't exactly out of the goodness of their hearts, I'm ashamed to say. They felt obligated to take Marie in. Her parents were my parents' oldest friends. They were in a car crash, and only Marie survived. Mother said people would gossip and dislike our family if we didn't step up and take her in. Daddy loves children and always does whatever Mother tells

him too, so he just nodded and went to pick Marie up from the hospital. She was 16. She and I argue constantly, partly because Mother always pitted us against each other and partly because we're so different. She drives me crazy, but my heart breaks for her. She lost her parents so young.

Before she had time to stop or censor herself, Erin had sent a reply.

BlackVelvetBitches: Yeah, being an orphan's a bitch.

IsabellaMartinez1: I'm sorry to have brought up such a painful subject, but I suppose we were going to get there at some point. Would you tell me your story?

Erin laughed mirthlessly. It sounded cold and desperate in the empty apartment. Clearly, she wasn't going to be allowed to cheer up tonight.

BlackVelvetBitches: I can't. Not right now. I promise, I'll tell you sometime soon. I'm just having a shitty night, and I think I need to be alone for a while. Sorry.

There was a long pause. Erin tried to relax her tense shoulders by rolling them but stopped. What was the point of trying to make herself feel better?

IsabellaMartinez1: No need to apologize. I understand. As I said, I'm sorry to have brought up something so painful. I hope you will tell me one day, though. Heaven knows I've burdened you with lots of details of my childhood. Funny that I didn't talk more about Marie when I spilled my guts to you. Maybe it was because I only lived with her for a year before I moved out. A psychologist would make a big deal out of me omitting her, I'm sure. Anyway, sorry to start talking again. I'll leave you alone.

Erin tried to relax her jaw and ignore the ache in her chest.

BlackVelvetBitches: Don't worry about it. Sorry again.

IsabellaMartinez1: Don't be. I just hope I didn't make your night worse somehow, Erin.

BlackVelvetBitches: It's not your fault. Not at all. Just chalk it up to me being a loner, or what was it you called it...introvert?

IsabellaMartinez1: Introvert, yes. All right. Well, good night. I hope you manage to sleep and that tomorrow is a better day for you.

BlackVelvetBitches: Thanks. 'Night.

Erin pushed the lid of her laptop down a little harder than she probably should have. Listlessly, she washed her face and brushed her teeth. Then she crawled into bed, and for the first time in over ten years, she cried herself to sleep.

Chapter 16

The Whole Package

IT HAD BEEN A PRODUCTIVE morning for Isabella, and she felt unusually energized. As she stood in line at the post office, waiting patiently for once, she felt rested and wondered if her sleep had improved. Not that she was sleeping more, but perhaps it was deeper. It seemed the only explanation for her alertness and ability to cope with the day.

Still, it didn't quite ring true, not since she'd been struggling with nightmares centered on her lackluster relationship and how she had no control over her life. It just trudged on without joy or purpose. Except, of course, for loving and raising Alberto.

She could no longer pretend her relationship with Richard didn't remind her of a dead houseplant in a window, still standing on the windowsill for everyone to see with its withered leaves and decaying roots—mocking the life and beauty it should possess.

Wryly, she realized that she could probably resurrect an actual plant with greater ease and more success than she could this relationship. She wasn't happy. Surely Richard wasn't happy either? He deserved to be loved, to be needed and appreciated. Talking to Erin had opened Isabella's eyes to that. How had she ignored the issue for so long?

She chewed the inside of her cheek. Was she actually sleeping better or merely feeling less depressed because of Erin's presence in her life? Speaking to her new friend, getting to know her, had injected energy and meaning back into her life. Was this what made her more alert and present?

"My, what a cute baby! He's so precious!" an old woman suddenly said, while staring into the stroller and grinning happily at Alberto.

Isabella forced a smile. Not much for pleasantries, she still had difficulties getting used to the friendly people of Florida.

"Thank you. He certainly is," she said, then turned in the direction of the post office clerk, a clear hint to the old woman that Isabella was done with the conversation. It didn't work.

"How old is he? What's the little angel's name?" chirped the old woman, still looking at Alberto.

Annoyed or not, Isabella felt the swelling of maternal pride, and charitably gave the woman another smile. "It's Alberto, and he is three months."

"What a sweet name for a sweet boy. And all that hair! He's going to charm the girls."

"And the boys," Isabella added nonchalantly.

The old lady looked confused. "Pardon?"

"He'll charm all the girls and the boys. Oh, and the people who don't feel like either category, too. I'm certain he'll win over anyone he wants to charm." Isabella wasn't just trying to make a point; she hoped the subject would make the other woman less inclined to keep talking. That didn't work either.

Instead, the pensioner beamed. "Of course! Have 'em all. That's what I say! No one ever told me I could choose anything else when I was a girl. Could you imagine having options? Personally, I'd go with one of them people who have both sets of parts. Call me greedy, but I think I'd like to have both. And all of it in one person…well, saves time. Dating takes so much time. Especially at my age, when you have to nap so much."

Isabella stared at the woman, relieved to find her so open-minded but unsure what to say next. Where should she start? Should she try to teach this old lady about not fetishizing whole groups of people? Should she laugh at the "frequent naps" thing? The old lady wasn't looking at her, though. She was busy trying to get Alberto to wave at her.

Isabella was saved, as she was called to the window. She said goodbye to the woman, then handed the clerk the package for Erin and asked to get it sent ASAP.

In the package was, as promised, half her bag of Azúcar Negra, and a little something else, something much more valuable that she'd gone out to buy a few hours ago. It had taken a long time to find exactly what she was looking for, but just shy of eleven, she'd found it and added it to the package.

Isabella hoped Erin wouldn't balk at the pricey gift, nor the money she was forking over to have it sent express delivery. As far as she was concerned, Erin deserved a real treat.

She was also sending the proofread and printed copy of how she met Richard and ended up where she was today. That made Isabella painfully nervous.

She paid and thanked the man before turning the stroller around and walking out into the sunshine. The old woman waved to Alberto as she passed, but Isabella was too preoccupied to react. She was trying to analyze why she felt so comfortable talking about her dreams and fears to Erin but not about how she met her boyfriend, nor how she longed to leave him.

Was it because even she could see the hesitation and regret in those words? No matter how she'd edited, her explanation still showed that she'd settled for what seemed clinically logical. The best choice for Alberto, not for her. And certainly not for Richard. She didn't love Richard. Not romantically, anyway. Did she really want to raise Alberto in a home where his parents were just pretending to be a couple?

Surely Erin would see it like that. Would she judge her? Judge her for settling for a safe situation? For focusing on Alberto's needs because her own didn't matter? *Was I born disliking myself? Or is my own disregard for my happiness and needs something else to blame on my mother?*

Isabella gritted her teeth until her jaw ached. She had to contain her emotions. She was in public, and she was with Alberto. Even though he was too young to understand, Isabella hated the idea of him seeing her upset. She wanted to be strong and calm for him. Tears started to form in her eyes, and she growled with anger. She walked more quickly to the car, molding her fears and doubts into anger. Anger she could deal with.

Focusing on what had to be done, she gritted her teeth and got on with it. She was going to go home, feed Alberto, and prepare lunch for herself. At least Richard was at work today, and she didn't have to worry if there was enough for them both. She felt increasingly ashamed and confused that his presence only annoyed her.

It had been so strange when Richard wasn't out somewhere with Joshua. Having him home for the weekend had just made her doubts stronger. All the jokes he made that weren't funny, but still she felt she had to laugh. Or when she felt guilty, because she wished he wasn't there. The times he would ask how Alberto liked this or that, proving he barely knew his son. Every moment made her skin crawl.

Poor Richard. What have I dragged him into? She resented the thought the second it arose. He was a grown man. He could take responsibility for himself. Couldn't he?

Her knuckles had turned white on the handles of the stroller. She had to stop thinking about this right now. She could berate herself later, when she was at home and away from Alberto.

She thought about the package, soon to be on its way to New York, and hoped with every fiber of her being it would coax out one of those infectious, Erin Black smiles. And, yes, she hoped she would be allowed to see that smile. She had to admit, just to herself, how much she wanted to see her again. Erin had a way of making everything seem clearer…more manageable. She calmed her.

Isabella wished she could be on Skype. To look into Erin's honest, sea-green eyes and find her answers in them.

She got herself, the stroller, and Alberto safely into the car and drove home. She had a baby to feed, lunch to make, and a lot of soul searching to do.

Oh, and the kitchen cupboards had to be cleaned. With a sigh, she decided that keeping busy was probably the best thing to do. At least until she could figure out what to do about everything else.

The afternoon sun hid behind the clouds. Isabella watched them drift across the sky with Alberto in her arms. It was almost time for his nap, but Isabella couldn't tear herself away. Looking at the clouds made her problems seem less pressing.

She looked down at Alberto, lying snugly in her arms, as he peered up at her.

"Alberto, we need to talk about your dad. I know, I arranged everything so that you would have a mommy and a daddy and a safe place to grow up. But here's the problem, cariño. I'm not happy with your father. And I'm starting to wonder if I might not be doing you any favors by going on like a robot, just going through the motions and not feeling anything. So what should I do?"

He gurgled and blinked at her. She gave him a tired smile.

"That really wasn't helpful, you know. Maybe I should just forget what I want? Stick to the plan, and just give you your family? Although, maybe you'd like it if your family was just you and me, with occasional visits from your dad? Would that be okay? Would it be better for you if you didn't see your dad so much but your mom was happy? Is that selfish? So many questions and so few answers."

Alberto started cooing and reached his hand out to grab the tip of her nose. Her laugh as he caught it sounded more like a sob.

"That's right, *mi príncipe*. You work on your coordination. It's my job to worry about everything else. Let's try and get you to sleep."

Isabella felt tired but was too anxious to rest. She rocked Alberto to sleep, then put him in his baby bouncer and watched him sink into a comfortable position. The bouncer was right by her writing desk in the corner of the living room, so she could keep an eye on him as she wrote. The only problem with this arrangement was that, on rare occasions, the tapping of the keys woke him. She'd have to risk it; today, she felt like she could write, and she didn't want to waste that.

As she booted up the PC, she realized that talking to Erin made her feel more creative too. Perhaps it was a side effect from the increased energy, she mused.

For the hundredth time, she wondered why she'd become so attached to Erin. Was it simply because she needed something—someone—new in her life, because she was unhappy with Richard? Would—could—someone else have the same effect on her?

She considered Erin and all the other people she had met online while tweeting and on Facebook, people who lived close by, attractive men, people she had more in common with. None of them had interested her. No, there was something about Erin that caught her interest, and more importantly, kept it. There was something about her that woke Isabella up. Something about Erin had changed her—changed everything.

That change made Isabella face what was right in front of her and had been for quite some time, a family that wasn't a true family. They were simply two adults sharing a house and loving the same child. Richard could be a good partner and a good father, but not to her and Alberto. *And he deserves so much better than what I'm giving him. I owe it to him to let him know that.*

They were so out of sync. Surely that wasn't right for anyone. She couldn't just go through the motions anymore. She had to make a decision, one that wasn't influenced by Erin or even made solely for Alberto's sake. It had to be a decision that was the lesser of two evils for Richard, Alberto, and her. Was she sick with the worry that she was making the wrong decision? Yes. But she'd spent plenty of time in her career having to make unpleasant decisions. Do we cut back on personnel or on materials? Do we invest further or stay the course? Do we take a gamble on more exotic cuisine, or do we stick to what we know works? Do I leave Richard or find a way to live in a loveless relationship?

She could find the right solution they could all live with. She had to. It was then she realized just how distanced she was from Richard. Until that moment, it never occurred to her that he should be involved in making this decision, that he could help if she talked to him. But then, he had never given any indication that he wanted anything to change.

Have I? Haven't we both just let things run their course with sad smiles and empty kisses?

It was all so complicated, so many gray areas and endless, seemingly unanswerable questions. Her stomach ached, and her jaw hurt from grinding her teeth again.

Who did she think she was kidding? In the past, Isabella had had no qualms about who she'd had to lie to in order to achieve her goals. But she never, ever lied to herself. That was the line she wouldn't cross. And she wouldn't—couldn't—start now. She and Richard weren't working. They were never going to work. Seeing the effect Erin had on her had proved that without a doubt.

Nevertheless, her future with or without Richard needed to be decided without Erin factoring into the equation. Richard deserved that, at least.

They had a son together, after all. One way or another, they would always be in each other's lives because of Alberto. And he was a good man. He was kind and sweet and gentle. He just wasn't right for her. She wasn't right for him. They both deserved more than they were prepared to give each other. And Alberto deserved a father who could give him the love and attention he deserved. Isabella had to believe that if she and their broken relationship were not standing in the way, Richard would be a more attentive father.

Exhausted by relentless musings that seemed to go on in never-ending circles, she sat down to write, in the hope that it would block it all out for a while.

Eventually, the words began to flow. Her shoulders relaxed, as did her jaw muscles, as she escaped her own life for a while and delved into the world of fairy tales. Next to her, Alberto slept, his little hands opening and closing with his dreams.

The afternoon had flown by in a blissful writing frenzy and time spent playing with Alberto. The subsequent dinner with Richard was polite and quick, since he excused himself to go out for drinks with an old friend.

But no matter how short the time, it had still felt like torture to Isabella. She constantly cast wary glances at him. Her pulse raced, and her appetite was nonexistent. She felt like she was betraying him in one moment, and freeing him from equal misery in the next. She recalled that Richard had promised he would always be there for them, that he would never make the mistakes he'd made with Shay and Joshua, and that he would never leave her. She believed he meant every word. He would stay by her side, no matter how miserable they both were, because he'd promised her he would. She could release him from that promise. She could let him go. Should she set them both free? Could she?

The three hours spent talking to Erin about movies, TV shows, and books were glorious. Leaving the chat was a painful decision, but she was bone tired. The words had begun to swim into one big alphabet soup on her screen, forcing her to say good night. She was learning that mental anguish and uncertainty really were exhausting.

She cuddled up in her chair, pulled her blankets around herself, and looked over at the sleeping Alberto one last time, to make sure he was all right. Then she closed her eyes and drifted into a deep sleep.

One second, she felt herself descending into sleep. The next, she felt small, hard pebbles under her bare feet.

Isabella looked around. Where was she? A beach? She knew this place. A vague memory grew stronger in her dreaming mind. With effort, she remembered visiting that beach early one spring with her parents. How old had she been—five, six maybe? She couldn't quite remember, but in the dream it didn't much matter. She remembered how she had been dragged along for a trip to see several scenic parts of northern Europe with her parents. They had visited some fellow bourgeois Americans who had emigrated.

In the dream, she began to walk. The feel of the small pebbles and the look of the gray sky and the ocean, so dark that it was almost black, brought back more memories. She remembered taking off her shoes because her mother had said she wasn't allowed to. She'd told her that she would hurt her feet. Sadly, her mother hadn't seen the tiny rebellion. She had been too busy walking ahead with the American art collector who was playing host to them all. Where was her father? She couldn't remember. Strangely, she could remember the art collector talking about the unique light and the quaint towns and ruins that were 'just to die for'—or maybe her adult mind filled that in—but she couldn't remember her father being part of the scene. She found herself wondering what that meant. Did it mean anything? Was it just an idiosyncrasy of her adult dreaming mind or of deeper significance to her undeveloped child mind? She couldn't remember him being there, because he never truly was. Not when she needed him. Not when she needed his protection.

The cliff face in front of her drew her attention away from her musing, and her eyes followed it up to the solitary church at the top. It looked stark and abandoned. She wasn't sure if it had actually been on that beach or if it was part of her dream. She supposed it didn't matter.

Little Isabella had hated the trip. She had wanted to be home with her toys, home where she didn't have to travel constantly from one hotel room to the next. Home was where there weren't so many new faces all the time and where the food didn't taste so strange. Home was where people spoke English and didn't laugh at her when she didn't understand the ways of foreign cultures.

The sudden, overwhelming urge that she was supposed to be searching for someone overtook her. She heard her mother's voice calling her from behind. Chasing her. She turned to answer, to tell her she had to find… someone…but her mother wasn't there. It was just her voice, sharp and echoing in her ear—loud, urgent, yet unintelligible. Isabella ran. Her feet pounding, slapping against the stones. The pebbles hurt her feet. She looked down, checking to see where she was going, but they were no longer a child's feet. They were her feet as they looked now, full grown and aching with every pounding step.

Still, she heard her mother's voice. Speaking so fast—too fast—for Isabella to clearly make out the words. Straining as she ran, all she could decipher were the words *failure* and *disappointment.* No surprise there, she thought in her dream. But it didn't calm her. That disembodied voice hunted her, and she just couldn't shake it.

Her lungs ached from the cold air she sucked into her body as she continued to run. She tried to take calm, deep breaths, but the air, heavy with the scent of seaweed, salt, and something which reminded her of lavender, bit and clung inside her, refusing to replenish her body with much-needed oxygen, as she pounded down the beach,

Still, she searched. She didn't know who she was looking for. But she could feel it, sense it. If she found them, her mother's voice would let her go..

Isabella ran to the end of the beach, the cliff with the lonely church towering above her. She saw a trickling waterfall to her right, more like a small brook dribbling down the rocky wall than an actual waterfall. She remembered putting her hand in it and the feel of the cold water splashing on her clothes when she reached in and touched the squishy, thick, blue clay covering the rock face underneath.

In the dream, however, there was a man under the waterfall. When she reached out her hand, she didn't touch the clay. She touched his face. She yelped and jumped back, then watched, frozen to the spot, as he stepped out from the cliff. He was perfectly dry, as if the water hadn't even touched him.

He was a man in his twenties, she guessed. She didn't know him. But yet…somehow…she did. She knew him like she knew herself, but not who he was. She wanted to ask him, only to find a strangling fear stopping her.

As she watched the familiar stranger, his face contorted in pain.

"Why did you do it?"

"Do what?" Isabella asked.

"Why did you make me grow up without him?"

She woke with a start, gripping the armrests of her chair so tight that she made the armrests creak.

Her waking mind dissolved the features of the man, blurred them until all she was left with was the image of his eyes seared into her, those beautiful, blue-green eyes.

She turned to the crib. Alberto was sleeping soundly. His eyes—the ones she had just seen in her dream—were firmly closed.

Her hands were clammy, as she forced her fingers to release the armrests before wiping them off on her pajama bottoms. Her breath was coming in too fast, and she felt as if she couldn't get enough oxygen.

She snuck toward the window and opened it with minimal noise.

It was silent out there. The blowing breeze ruffled her hair. The fresh air was soothing, and she breathed it in greedily. Fresh oxygen and the bracing chill did their magic. Waves of dizziness ebbed away like the receding tide on the beach.

Eventually, her breathing calmed, but her mind didn't. It couldn't. Images from the dream haunted her. Thoughts of the past, present, and future blurred in a cyclone of confused pictures and disjointed thoughts. She needed distraction.

She closed the window and tiptoed silently back to her chair. When she was cozy under her blanket, she picked up her iPad.

Her fingers hovered over the Skype app. Erin was an insomniac and had said she wasn't at all tired when Isabella had left the chat. There was a good chance she was still up and online.

The only problem was that it felt selfish to try and contact Erin now. She should be leaving her alone so that Erin would go to bed and at least try for some sleep.

Rubbing at her forehead, Isabella felt worry lines forming. Everything made Isabella feel selfish right now. She looked over at Alberto. Guilt wrapped its serpentine coils about her, constricting her throat. She struggled to swallow. She had to escape this feeling. And the only thing she could think of was to talk to someone. So she typed quietly but hurriedly.

IsabellaMartinez1: Erin? Are you awake?

A few seconds ticked by, as she stared at the screen. Isabella was about to give up and read an e-book or something instead. A message popped up, almost cutting her already frayed nerves to ribbons.

BlackVelvetBitches: Hey Ms. Writer. :) Yep, I'm here. I was on Twitter, so I nearly missed your message. Why aren't you asleep?

Isabella stared at the words. What was she going to say? "I had a bad dream. Please make me feel better?" Ridiculous.

IsabellaMartinez1: I woke up again and don't seem to be able to go back to sleep.

BlackVelvetBitches: Aww, sorry to hear that. Good for me, though. I get more of your company. Yay!

IsabellaMartinez1: I wouldn't celebrate. I'm not sure I'll be good company.

BlackVelvetBitches: Don't be silly. You're always great to have around.

Isabella was far too fragile for Erin to be this sweet to her. She might cry or wail like a banshee. Or both. But she was a Martinez, so all that was off the table. She had to control herself.

IsabellaMartinez1: You're very kind. Have you tried for any sleep?

BlackVelvetBitches: Nope, I'm starting to feel tired but not settled enough to get some z's. Actually, it's past midnight, but I might still spring for some coffee now that my midnight-coffee buddy is here.

IsabellaMartinez1: Should I be telling you to go to bed?

BlackVelvetBitches: Whoa, way to show your mom credentials, there. You can't send me to bed. I'm too big and too far away.

IsabellaMartinez1: Fine. You get to stay up. This time. One night, however, you might just find me at your door with a glass of hot milk and a bedtime story.

BlackVelvetBitches: Hey, that actually sounds kinda nice. Especially if there's some honey and whiskey in the milk and the bedtime story is a raunchy lesbian detective story.

IsabellaMartinez1: Oh, really, Miss Black? Read many of those?

BlackVelvetBitches: Nope. Not much of a reader. Unless it's comics, of course. But you could read me stuff and I'd listen. Don't tell anyone...but I really like your voice.

Isabella felt unexpected heat in her cheeks.

IsabellaMartinez1: That's nice to hear. Thank you.

BlackVelvetBitches: This could all be in my head, but your replies seem shorter and less teasing than normal. You okay?

Isabella sighed and shook her head. When had she become this transparent?

IsabellaMartinez1: Honestly? No, not really. This sounds silly, but I had a particularly rough nightmare.

BlackVelvetBitches: Doesn't sound silly at all. Nightmares can be your brain throwing your worst crap right in your face. With added monsters and nothing making sense. It's friggin' awful. Some of the worst experiences of my life have been in dreams, and dude...that's saying something.

IsabellaMartinez1: Sounds like you have a lot of experience, then?

BlackVelvetBitches: I went through periods with lots of night terrors as a kid. Especially when I got a new group home or a temporary placement with a foster family. The first week was basically my brain torturing me. Didn't help my insomnia one bit. Luckily, the dreams got less intense when I hit puberty.

Isabella bit her lip.

IsabellaMartinez1: I'm not sure I should be telling you about my problems. I feel like I have no right to complain when I compare our lives. Perhaps I should just ask you to tell me one of your awful jokes.

BlackVelvetBitches: Really? Coz I heard a great one on the radio. It goes like this: If you ever get cold, why don't you stand in the corner for a bit—they're usually 90 degrees. Ba-bom tssh.

That didn't make Isabella feel any better.

IsabellaMartinez1: Right. Thanks for the effort. But I'm afraid that did nothing but make me roll my eyes.

BlackVelvetBitches: Yeah...I thought that might be the case. Why don't you just tell me what you dreamt?

IsabellaMartinez1: Like I said, I feel like I shouldn't.

BlackVelvetBitches: Oh, come on. I'm asking, aren't I? Besides, it's not a who-had-the-worst-life competition. You seem to be the one who is going through the worst stuff right now. So, you know, vent. Get it off your chest. Lean on me, gorgeous.

IsabellaMartinez1: All right. It was a strange dream. But then they always are, I suppose. I was at a beach where my family traveled one spring, when I was little. I was miserable there as a child and just as miserable in the dream, even though I was an adult this time. My mother's voice kept chasing me, but she wasn't there. Other than that, everything was the same as in the memory. Oh, except that I wasn't there with my mother and her friend like I was in the memory. I was alone. And an adult. And I was looking for someone.

Isabella hit *send* to break the message up and make it more readable. It was only then she read what she had written. What was that gibberish? She groaned softly. What was wrong with her? She always checked her messages before she sent them. She could only blame the panic that was still lodged deep in her chest.

> **IsabellaMartinez1:** I just re-read that and saw that I explained that I was an adult twice. And barely made any sense. My apologies. I'm still a bit shaken up.

> **BlackVelvetBitches:** Never mind. It's okay. Just tell me about the dream.

> **IsabellaMartinez1:** Everything was so bleak, and I was so stressed by my mother's voice. It was just behind me, just out of reach. And I couldn't hear what it was saying, other than a few words about disappointment and failure. But for some reason, I knew that if I found who I was looking for, the voice would go away.

Isabella ran her hands over her face. How much detail should she go into? She already felt bad about how she was constantly confiding in Erin, constantly complaining.

> **IsabellaMartinez1:** Then I came across the person I needed to find. I think it was Alberto, but he was all grown up. He said that I had made a decision that ruined his childhood.

> **BlackVelvetBitches:** See what I mean about dreams? Your mom never leaving you alone and your son suffering coz you did something wrong. Your brain knows your worst fears and it was just playing you a nice little horror film of 'em. I know it doesn't help right now. But when you calm down, knowing that might just make you feel better.

IsabellaMartinez1: Yes, I'm sure you're right. You're also right in that this was a rather transparent dream. Pretty literal, really. So much for my creative mind.

BlackVelvetBitches: Hey, don't be so hard on your brain. It was sleeping, okay? Cut it some slack.

Isabella stifled a laugh, worried about waking Alberto. The cold grip of panic was starting to let go of her throat.

IsabellaMartinez1: How do you always manage to make things better?

BlackVelvetBitches: I sold my spleen to the devil for good comforting skills. I tried to sell my soul, but the devil said he already had three of those.

It was calming to know that Erin's jokes were still as bad and still as cute. Isabella couldn't quite stop a snigger this time. She looked over at Alberto. He was still sleeping. She looked at the screen for a heartbeat or two, before deciding to open up.

IsabellaMartinez1: Erin. The decision that I made, the one that Alberto seemed so pained about? It was leaving his father.

There was a long pause. Isabella didn't blame her. She didn't know what she would have said if she was in Erin's shoes.

BlackVelvetBitches: Huh. Okay. Well, as I said, it's just your brain showing you the worst-case scenario.

IsabellaMartinez1: Yes, I know. Which means it's a real fear, a real dilemma that I must deal with.

BlackVelvetBitches: Can I tell you something? Or is there more about the dream you need to get out?

Isabella tilted her head as she looked at the message. Where could this be going?

IsabellaMartinez1: No, go ahead.

BlackVelvetBitches: There was this foster home I stayed in for a while. The foster parents were nice. Loved kids, absolutely adored each and every one of us. It looked perfect on paper. There was just the small matter of the fact that they didn't love each other so much. Or maybe they just didn't like each other. Either way, they fought like cats and dogs. And when they didn't fight, they avoided each other. It made the whole house totally uncomfortable. All us kids were on edge, wondering when the next fight was going to start, what would set it off this time. Even if we didn't see them fight, we knew they were miserable with each other. We felt it. It made us all…kinda wary and cautious, I guess. We didn't trust the times when they seemed happy, because we knew it wouldn't last. And we learned not to trust them, because every time they told us they loved each other, we knew they were lying to us. So how could we believe a word they said? I'm not saying that you and Richard would ever be like that, but if there is this weirdness between you, Alberto will feel it. Kids don't understand grown-up stuff, but they pick up vibes. And bad vibes can be scary as hell when you don't understand what they are.

IsabellaMartinez1: I hadn't thought about that.

BlackVelvetBitches: You see things differently when you grow up like I did. You see a lot of adults trying their best but failing in so many different ways. That's not to say that there weren't adults who got it right too. I had some amazing social workers and foster parents who I'll be eternally grateful to. Anyway, there's another side to your problem.

IsabellaMartinez1: There is?

BlackVelvetBitches: Yep. Once again, I'm no expert on how to raise a kid right. But it seems to me that it would be easier to teach a kid how to be happy and to be true to themselves if you were those things? Sorry, did that make sense? It's late and the words don't seem to be explaining what I'm thinking very well. :)

IsabellaMartinez1: No, that was perfectly clear. If I'm content and live my life the way I want to, it will be easier to teach Alberto to achieve that in his own life.

BlackVelvetBitches: Exactly! Basically, I think that happy parents are better parents. But what the hell do I know, right?

IsabellaMartinez1: I think you know more than you give yourself credit for. An outsider's view of a family can be very insightful, obviously. Thank you, Erin. You've made me feel a lot calmer.

BlackVelvetBitches: Don't sweat it. I'm glad I could help. I feel like I should add that I'm not telling you what to do here. I'm just saying that if you do leave Richard, it's not necessarily gonna make your nightmare come true. Kids grow up without their dad around 24/7 all the time, and I'm sure he'd still be in Alberto's life lots and lots. Wouldn't he?

IsabellaMartinez1: Yes. I think he would. I hope so at least.

BlackVelvetBitches: There you go, then. You'll make the right decision for lil' man, because you love him and you worry about what's best for him. Oh, and you'll never go on holiday with your mom again, so that part of the dream won't come true either. ;-)

IsabellaMartinez1: No, that's for sure. Again, thank you for reassuring me.

BlackVelvetBitches: And, once again, not a problem. Feel like you can sleep now?

Isabella sighed as she took stock. She was calmer now, and things were looking a little less bleak. But shutting her thoughts off enough for sleep? Not a chance.

IsabellaMartinez1: No, I'm afraid my brain wouldn't allow that. The annoying thing is far too busy playing out scenarios and reminding me of the panic of my dream.

BlackVelvetBitches: Okay, well, we can keep chatting. That'll distract you.

Alberto made a noise, somewhere between a mewl and a grunt. Isabella looked over at him. He was moving about, showing every sign of not sleeping so soundly anymore.

IsabellaMartinez1: I'd love to. However, I think we both need to try for some sleep. You have work tomorrow, and I should be at least a little rested for when Alberto wakes up. I just wish I could have some alcohol or medicine to quiet my mind. Damn breastfeeding.

She saw the little pen that showed that Erin was typing. But no message seemed to come. Either this was an extremely long message, or Erin wasn't sure whether to press *send* or not. Finally, a message appeared.

BlackVelvetBitches: I've got something that might help you. Unless you think it's silly. I've sort of collected lots of tricks on how to fool your brain to sleep. I've been asking people and reading about it online over the years.

IsabellaMartinez1: But none of them work for you?

BlackVelvetBitches: Usually not, no. I'm immune to sleep. ;-)

IsabellaMartinez1: Well, I'm not. So, if you want to share a tip or two, I'd be glad to hear them.

BlackVelvetBitches: Okay. I'll share the one that does sometimes work for a tough case like me. Just don't laugh, okay?

Isabella wasn't sure if she should feel offended or just sorry for Erin.

IsabellaMartinez1: Of course I won't. I laugh with you, never at you.

BlackVelvetBitches: Yeah, I know. It's just that this is really personal stuff, you know? What I'm gonna tell you isn't the usual stuff about counting to a hundred backward or focusing on making your out-breaths as long as your in-breaths. I'm gonna tell you my way of trying to shut my brain down and get into sleep mode. It might be a bit weird.

IsabellaMartinez1: I'm sure it's not. Besides, even if it was, I'd never tease you about it. Especially not now that I know you are sensitive about this issue. Don't worry, you're safe with me.

BlackVelvetBitches: Okay. I have a thing I kinda...imagine right before I sleep. First of all, are you afraid of tight spaces?

IsabellaMartinez1: No, I've never been claustrophobic.

BlackVelvetBitches: Good. So, you're in bed. Lying comfortably and ready to sleep. That's when you imagine that you're out walking late at night. It's a safe place, no one around. The starlight makes it cozy and pretty. There are crickets in the background, but that's the only noise you hear. You're heading for a hole in the ground which is covered by a lid. You open the lid and step into the hole, closing the lid above you, closing out the world and all your waking thoughts. It's totally silent in there. The hole is lit up only by dim, warm, yellow light. There's a ladder, and you start climbing down it. You know you're safe, and you're climbing down to a place that's even safer. It gets warmer and toastier as you climb down the ladder. The light dims too. The comfortable warmth and dim light makes you tired. With every step down the ladder, you get more relaxed, and your breaths get longer and deeper. When you are so far down that it's almost completely dark, you find yourself in a hollow. It's lit by a single candle. There's a clean mattress on the ground. It's really big and thick and comfortable. On it are your favorite pillows, duvets, and blankets. Whatever makes you the coziest—it's there on that mattress, waiting for you to snuggle up. So that's what you do. Slowly and easily, so you don't stop being sleepy. Your bed smells faintly like vanilla and Christmas spices. Lovely and welcoming. Your long, deep breaths...fill your lungs with it. There is a vent hole somewhere, because the air still feels fresh and full of oxygen. You have never felt so safe or snuggly before. You're, like, cocooned in this warm, dark, safe place. As you feel how soft and perfect everything is, that single candle slowly dies out. When it's dark in the little hollow, you fall into deep, restful sleep.

Isabella read the words and felt her eyes wanting to close.

IsabellaMartinez1: That was almost hypnotic. I feel like I'm about to fall asleep.

BlackVelvetBitches: Oh cool! So, it's not silly or weird to you?

IsabellaMartinez1: No. I mean, I could poke holes in the scenario if I were to think about it logically. However, that's obviously not the point here. It's seems like a good way to relax and to keep unwanted thoughts at bay. Very clever, Miss Black.

BlackVelvetBitches: Shush, you'll make me go red. Anyway, if you think that might work, you shouldn't sit here talking to me. You should go and use it while you still feel sleepy.

IsabellaMartinez1: You're probably right. Are you going to go try it too?

BlackVelvetBitches: Sure. Why not? I'm actually starting to feel tired now.

IsabellaMartinez1: Let's try it, then. Thank you so much for your help tonight. I appreciate it more than I can say.

BlackVelvetBitches: Stop thanking me. I was glad I could help. :-) Talk sometime tomorrow?

IsabellaMartinez1: Absolutely. Good night, Erin.

BlackVelvetBitches: Good night. Sweet dreams.

Isabella read the scenario about the hole in the ground once more, making sure she remembered the gist of it at least. Then she put her iPad down and pulled her blanket up to her chin. She started to imagine walking out into the woods on a warm summer's night, heading for that hole in the ground. She imagined the climb down and getting into the little nest of soft bedding. She made her breathing slower and deeper with every step, just as Erin had said. She could almost feel different parts of her brain shutting down, as she focused on the simple scenario. When she imagined being on the cozy mattress and the candle burning out, she fell asleep.

The second she was asleep, the relaxation scenario changed to a dream. A dream where Erin was with her in that mass of bedding in the underground hollow, lying behind her, spooning her gently, and breathing warmly against her neck. It was the nicest dream Isabella had experienced in years.

Chapter 17

The Unavoidable Chat

Monday was a busy day, and for once, Erin was happy about it. She threw herself into her work, and she enjoyed talking to people—weird for an introvert usually drained by polite small talk and speaking to strangers. Today, however, she was happy for anything to keep her mind off Isabella and the fact that she should probably stop talking to her.

Her body was eager to move, as if it were trying to take over from her brain and heart, the causes of her agony. Every chance she got, she exercised; her blood coursed through her like hot rivers, as her muscles flexed. It was so easy. She only had to envisage herself doing the move and then do it. Her muscles, tendons, and nerve endings followed her orders and completed the motion. If only everything in life was as straightforward.

Still, the workday ended, and eventually she had to go home. When she entered the apartment, her laptop was perched on the table, taunting her; pushing her and stabbing at wounds that hurt enough already.

She should've eaten out somewhere—anywhere. She put her jacket back on and hit the stairs. She was nearly dead from exhaustion by the time she reached the ground floor.

Deciding against the subway, she took a slow walk to cool down and ended up outside a fast-food place. She put aside all pretense that she was even going to try to eat healthily tonight.

When she'd finished her giant burger, she sipped her drink while watching the people around her. Most of them were talking to each other or busy on their phones. The unbidden knowledge that she had the Skype app on her phone popped into her mind. She could talk to Isabella right now, if she was online, of course.

Erin squeezed her eyes shut and groaned inwardly. Even if she did, what would she say? She couldn't just ask for a video chat and sit there and stare at Isabella. She'd have to talk to her, which meant it was decision time: either keep in touch and hope that her crush faded, or tell Isabella how she felt and stop talking to her. Neither option appealed. *Should've just stayed lonely, kept my head down, and not started talking to her.*

She was getting bored, and all the happy people talking to each other were bringing her down even more. It was time to go home and turn on the damn laptop. Whatever happened next, well, she'd just have to deal with it. Like always.

Slowly, she worked up the nerve to go home, turn on the laptop, make some coffee, and open Skype. After all that, Isabella wouldn't even be online yet. She assumed it was still far too early, being only 8 p.m.

She walked over to the apartment's only bookshelf and ran her finger across a bunch of comics. Picking out *Batwoman Hydrology* and the first issue of *Bitch Planet*, she flopped down on the bed. When she'd finished both, knowing them almost by heart, she kept going through her collection. As she read, she listened for any notifications from her laptop. It was almost ten when it pinged. She dropped her comic on the floor in fright.

She picked it up and threw it on the sofa before hurrying to the table and sitting down.

IsabellaMartinez1: Good evening, Erin. Are you here?

For some reason, Erin could hear Isabella's voice saying those words inside her head and goose bumps erupted on her arms. She groaned at the involuntary response.

BlackVelvetBitches: Yeah. I'm here.

IsabellaMartinez1: Well, that's good news. I was hoping you would be online so that I wouldn't have to wait until midnight to talk to you.

Erin's heart pounded. Isabella, though cautious and polite as usual, seemed genuinely happy to see her. Erin bit her lower lip and decided to just go for it and ask the question her mind couldn't stifle.

BlackVelvetBitches: You'd have waited for me if I wasn't here?

The reply was lightning fast. Clearly, Isabella didn't even have to think about it. Or debate the honest response.

IsabellaMartinez1: Of course.

Erin's breath caught in her chest, and she suddenly felt warm. That reply couldn't be better. Then Isabella sent another message.

IsabellaMartinez1: If I'm to be uncomfortably honest, nothing except sleep and Alberto needing me would keep me from trying to talk to you. I've had to admit that to myself.

Erin made a squeaking noise and stared at the words, reading them over and over. In lieu of a response, Isabella sent another message.

IsabellaMartinez1: Was that inappropriate? I'm afraid my social skills are a bit rusty. Alberto's conversation doesn't exactly keep me in good practice. Most of his conversation consists of noises that sound like "mmmhhhhmm" or "dadadah." And vast amounts of crying, of course.

Despite her emotional state, Erin laughed.

BlackVelvetBitches: Look, I don't know what you're complaining about. That sounds like perfectly reasonable talk to me. Leave the kid alone. He's doing his best! :-P

IsabellaMartinez1: I'm sure he is. Nevertheless, I'm glad to be talking to you.

BlackVelvetBitches: Not as glad as I am. I've missed you.

She had sent the words without thinking about it. But as soon as she saw them—black, barefaced, unflinching little letters on a luminescent, bright-white screen currently being read by Isabella—she freaked out. She quickly typed another message.

> **BlackVelvetBitches:** Whoa, now look who's being inappropriate! Sorry 'bout that!

There was no reply. Erin flexed her biceps nervously. Over and over and over again. Until, thankfully, a message popped up on her screen.

> **IsabellaMartinez1:** No need to be sorry. I've missed you too.

Erin gave a happy yelp and punched the air. In the back of her mind, she knew it changed nothing. In fact, it might even complicate things further. But right now, she didn't care. Isabella had missed her. Missed *her*. And she was comfortable enough to admit it. Erin wanted to say something to lighten the mood and make Isabella comfortable.

> **BlackVelvetBitches:** Glad to hear it! I was worried you hated me for making you learn those stretches. :-D

> **IsabellaMartinez1:** No, the stretches will do me good. Besides, it was nice to finally see you.

Something suddenly dawned on Erin.

> **BlackVelvetBitches:** Oh yeah, I forgot. I've seen you more than you've seen me.

> **IsabellaMartinez1:** Yes, and it's hideously unfair.

Erin chuckled as she typed her reply.

> **BlackVelvetBitches:** Are you pouting? I imagine you pouting.

> **IsabellaMartinez1:** Well, then I'm sure you're now imagining me rolling my eyes at you, as that is what I'm doing.

> **BlackVelvetBitches:** Fine! I won't mock you and your pouting. ;-) Let me make it up to you. Hmm, I can send you an embarrassing

picture of me? That way you get your revenge, and you will have seen about as much of me as I have of you. It'll be fair again!

IsabellaMartinez1: Tempting as that is, I have a better idea. But I'm not sure you're brave enough.

Erin furrowed her brow.

BlackVelvetBitches: Okay, well I'm always up for a challenge. Try me!

IsabellaMartinez1: What if I call you, and you have your camera on as we type to each other? Then I can see your facial expressions as you respond to what I write. But neither of us will talk, so we don't wake Alberto.

Erin chewed her lower lip. This was risky. What if Isabella could tell by her expressions or body language that she had a crush on her? But then, maybe that would be for the best? She wouldn't have to make the decisions if Isabella could just read it all on her face?

BlackVelvetBitches: All right. With one condition. After a while, you switch your camera on too!

There was a pause, and Erin wondered if Isabella was thinking that over or if Alberto had woken up.

IsabellaMartinez1: Deal. You're on camera for five minutes while we text chat, then I'll switch my camera on too. No sound, just writing and seeing each other's faces. My room will be poorly lit, I'm afraid, but that can't be helped.

BlackVelvetBitches: That's fine. I saw the lil' man well enough in that light, so I'm sure I'll see you too. The iPad will light you up a bit.

IsabellaMartinez1: Okay, I've switched the sound off. You can call me now.

Fear and excitement mingled in Erin's chest, the tendrils reaching down to take root in her stomach. She wondered what she looked like right now?

She'd showered at the gym and applied her usual sparse makeup after work, but that was hours ago, and the evening hadn't exactly been kind to her since. She thought up an excuse to go check.

BlackVelvetBitches: Hang on, I'm not quite decent. Let me go pick up a sweater.

IsabellaMartinez1: Oh. Yes, of course. Call when you're ready.

Erin hurried to the bathroom. She put some concealer on the rings under her eyes and tinted lip gloss on her pale lips. Spraying some of her Adidas perfume, she realized Isabella wouldn't be able to smell her. She was just freaking out. She hurried back and quickly threw a hoodie on over her shirt so that her excuse seemed legit.

BlackVelvetBitches: Right. Calling you now.

She clicked the button to make a video call. Part of her hoped that Isabella would have another technical fail and accidentally answer the call by clicking the camera button too, meaning that the video call would be shared right off the bat.

Sadly, Isabella knew what she was doing this time and clicked the button to answer normally. All Erin could see was Isabella's static profile picture and the little square on her screen showing her what Isabella could see, her own tired face. She muted her microphone so she couldn't wake the kid, not totally sure that Isabella had turned down her own sound properly.

IsabellaMartinez1: There you are, Miss Black. Decent now, I see. Might I ask what you were wearing before?

Erin was about to wince at her stupid lie. She now had to come up with a reason for why she hadn't been decent. Then she remembered the camera and turned the wince into a shy smile, one which came from the heart.

BlackVelvetBitches: Oh, you know. Just a tank top without a bra. No one needs to see that shit, so I covered up.

She stuck her tongue out toward the camera and grinned, not caring if the gesture was childish.

IsabellaMartinez1: Thank goodness you covered up. A woman in her late thirties like me can't be subjected to braless women. I've never seen one of those before. I could end up scarred for life.

BlackVelvetBitches: Chill, Captain Sarcasm-o! So, late thirties, huh? Wanna put an exact number on that?

IsabellaMartinez1: Not really, no.

BlackVelvetBitches: Oh, come on! Don't make me guess.

IsabellaMartinez1: I'm not telling you. And you can stop making that exasperated face. I can see you, remember?

Erin looked at the camera and gave it her most faked, toothpaste-ad smile.

BlackVelvetBitches: Better?

IsabellaMartinez1: It's an improvement, but it would be better with a real smile.

Erin looked down at the table, feeling suddenly shy. Then she took a deep breath and looked up at the camera, smiling in as heartfelt a manner as Isabella's presence usually inspired.

There was a long pause before Isabella replied, and Erin tried to cover her uneasiness by drinking some of her coffee. Then she was faced with a new problem—avoiding a grimace at how cold and bitter the coffee had gotten. She cursed at how bad she was at this sort of stuff.

IsabellaMartinez1: I hope you don't mind me saying this, Erin. But I really can't fathom how you can be single with a smile like that.

Erin stared at the words and forgot to breathe. Then she remembered that Isabella could see her and tried to defuse the situation by sticking her tongue out at the camera again.

IsabellaMartinez1: Ah, yes. Of course. That's the reason; you're childish and rude.

BlackVelvetBitches: I am not! You just make me nervous!

IsabellaMartinez1: Oh. I'm truly sorry. I don't mean to. I just can't seem to keep my thoughts and feelings to myself when I'm talking to you. I'm not usually this weak.

There was such intimacy and openness in those words that Erin was dumbstruck. She stared at the words and then straight into the camera, willing Isabella to look into her eyes and see what she was feeling.

Neither of them typed for a while. Erin wondered if Isabella was avoiding her gaze or if she was sitting there, in the Floridian evening, looking back and reading what was in Erin's eyes. Erin swallowed hard and broke the spell as she typed.

BlackVelvetBitches: Turn on your camera. Please. I need to see you.

Isabella didn't reply. But after a while, Erin's screen rearranged. Isabella's camera came on, and the screen filled with a dimly lit room and the face of the woman Erin had so quickly and unwillingly fallen in love with. Isabella swallowed visibly and tried for a smile, but it looked forced.

Erin licked her lips and then mouthed the word, "Hey."

This time, Isabella's smile looked real as she mouthed back, "Hello."

Goose bumps formed on Erin's arms again and on the back of her neck. Isabella seemed so close. She was right there. It felt like Erin could reach out, let her fingers go through the screen, and touch Isabella's cheek. It looked soft and warm, but then, all of Isabella looked soft and warm.

Isabella frowned a little and then looked down to type.

IsabellaMartinez1: Erin. What are we doing?

Erin looked at the words. Her heart pounded painfully hard, and her head swam. She had to decide right now. If she wanted to keep chatting every night and hope that her crush faded, she had to make a joke, break the tension, and talk about something else. If she wanted to tell Isabella how she felt...it had to be now.

Her hands shook over the keyboard.

> **BlackVelvetBitches:** I don't know. But I know that I'm kinda, you know, falling for you. Which is wrong! I know that. But I can't help it, and I don't know what to do.

She looked up, needing to see Isabella's face as she read those words.

Those beautiful features looked tense, almost afraid. Isabella looked up from the message, and for a few heartbeats, their eyes locked over the Internet connection. Then Isabella looked down to type before returning her gaze up to Erin's.

With trepidation, Erin looked down to read the reply.

> **IsabellaMartinez1:** I'm coming to terms with the fact that I feel the same, both when it comes to falling for you and not knowing what to do. I do know that I need to think about all of this. Until this moment, everything has been hypothetical. Now that I know there is something developing between us, I need to think about what that means. I have to consider Richard and Alberto. Would it be horrible of me to leave the chat now?

Erin swallowed hard again and looked up. She searched Isabella's face. She saw worry and doubt, but she wasn't looking at a woman so freaked out that she would never contact Erin again.

> **BlackVelvetBitches:** No. We both need to think about this. And I'm not gonna lie. After I've thrown up from an anxiety attack, I'll probably be ugly-dancing all over the apartment to celebrate that you like me.

She saw Isabella laugh on the screen, and her heart clenched. She had to type out her thoughts.

> **BlackVelvetBitches:** Fuck, you are so beautiful!

> **IsabellaMartinez1:** So are you. And don't call me "fuck." I have a name.

Erin chuckled at Isabella attempting to match her bad jokes and looked up at the screen to see Isabella try to hide a smug smile. She shook her head at the smiling woman and then looked down at her keyboard to type.

BlackVelvetBitches: So, I'll talk to you tomorrow?

IsabellaMartinez1: Yes. Oh, and there should be a package delivered to you tomorrow.

BlackVelvetBitches: Yay! Is it my coffee?

IsabellaMartinez1: Among other things. Erin, I'm going to hang up now. I'm far too overwhelmed by all of this.

BlackVelvetBitches: Of course. Night, Isabella.

Erin waved at the camera and smiled from ear to ear. Isabella looked hesitant as she typed.

IsabellaMartinez1: Good night, preciosa. I hope you sleep and have sweet dreams.

She looked back into the camera, blew Erin a kiss, and quickly hung up.

Erin got up and did a little dance and jumped high in the air a few times, and then, worrying about the neighbors, she whispered, "Yes, yes, yes, yes! She's into me!"

She looked up the word *preciosa* and loved that she had just been called precious. Then her heart sank, as she thought about the situation they were in. She remembered Isabella's typed words: *Now that I know there is something developing between us, I need to think about what that means. I have to consider Richard and Alberto.*

Erin shook her head. Isabella and Richard didn't have a relationship. Not a real one, anyway, and she'd done nothing wrong so far. There would be plenty of time for heartbreak and guilt. She should allow herself a few seconds of joy at that fact that she wasn't alone in these feelings. Maybe, there was some hope for a happy ending in the middle of all this awful mess, now that they were being honest with each other and thinking about the future.

The heavy rain outside smattered drum solos on her windows and made the apartment feel cozy, and Erin felt strangely calm. She went over to grab her phone from the bedside table. She needed to talk to someone. Not

Erika, someone less…sensible. Someone who wouldn't start talking about the issues and be negative.

She didn't want to concentrate on the problems right now. She needed to enjoy the moment. The only person she knew fitting that description—and who wouldn't think a text from her this late and out of the blue was weird—was Riley.

Erin frowned as she looked at her phone screen, weighing up how much of her relationship with Riley was friendship and how much was work. She did this every time they spoke, simply because Riley would always act as if they were best friends. But then, as soon as their workout was over, Erin usually didn't hear much from her. Still, it was only a text, not a vacation to Friendshipville.

Hey. I can't sleep and I need to talk to someone. You busy?

Instead of replying with a text, Riley called her. Erin grimaced. She hated when people called her in response to a nice, not-too-social text or e-mail conversation. She answered the call anyway. She heard Riley hollering hello and loud music in the background.

"Riley? Where the hell are you?"

"Where do you think I am? Turtle bingo? I'm at a club. Like you should be!"

Erin rolled her eyes. Maybe Riley hadn't been the best choice here. "You know what, Riles? Never mind. I'll blow off this excess energy playing online poker or something."

"Erin, come on. You said you always lose. I can talk to you for a bit. I promise not to pressure you to come out partying or socialize in any way. Pinky swear!"

Erin rolled her eyes but smiled despite herself. "Good. I need to talk about something amazing, complicated, and kinda scary."

"Sounds awesome. Well, except for the complicated part. Oh my God, do you know what I'm drinking?"

Erin slowly ran a hand over her face. "No, Riley, how the hell would I know that?"

"Dude, this is one of those fancy clubs where they do weird things in cocktails, and I just had three shots of whiskey with a chunk of actual honeycomb in each one. It was like an orgasm in my mouth."

"Riles. Ew, enough. I'm glad the shots were tasty. Now, you wanna hear my news or what?"

"Sorry, that was the alcohol and sugar rush talking there. Tell me everything!"

So Erin did. Her tale was less thought through and understandable than it had been when she had told Erika, and it had a lot more sound effects, but she told Riley all of it and then sat back to hear what the answer would be.

A wolf whistle was followed by, "Yeah, baby! You got the girl. Well, not yet, but I bet you're getting the girl as soon as she's single. Or, I mean, woman. Not girl. Whatever. Anyway, I can't believe you haven't told me that you were in the middle of a romance-novel situation here, babe."

Erin let out a sigh of relief. She'd needed someone to be more positive about this than she could allow herself to be.

"Is it?" she asked uncertainly.

"Hell yeah! Whatever happens next, you'll get it to work. She'll get rid of the beard and realize what's what. She clearly loves you and wants to have your little online babies."

Erin laughed. "Okay, I think you're exaggerating, but thanks for letting me be happy about this."

"Of course! Now, tell me… Do you call her Izzy, Isa, or Bella?"

Erin stifled a chuckle at the notion of trying to call the dignified Isabella Martinez either of those things. "None of the above. She's not a nickname kinda gal."

"So she's pretentious, huh?"

Her brows knitted. "Riley!"

"Okay, okay. Sorry. So, what does she look like?"

Erin smiled as she lay down on the bed, closed her eyes to picture Isabella, then described her in such detail that it was if she'd spent years looking at Isabella Martinez' face.

Chapter 18

Decisions and Cognac

Isabella rubbed her temples. The stress of her situation and the sudden fatigue were giving her a tension headache. Her head was throbbing badly, and she knew that painkillers would not help, nor would she be able to sleep until the throbbing abated.

Feeling increasingly restless and cooped up, Isabella snuck downstairs. She made coffee and watched as it filtered through, thinking about Erin the whole time. She thought about how lovely Erin had looked. About the shy smiles and the way that child of a woman stuck out her tongue.

She poured the coffee into her little cup and. for once, topped it up with cold water. She wanted to drink it soon, before her mind wasn't content to think just about Erin, before it went on to the more serious subjects of Richard, Alberto, and their life together.

When she'd drunk the coffee and thought up things she could say to make Erin smile for her again, she looked around the empty kitchen, her hands fidgeting restlessly. There had to be something to clean or rearrange before she went upstairs to check on Alberto

She decided go through the cabinets and get rid of foodstuff that might be past its expiration date. She started with the cupboard where they kept soft drinks and their sparse collection of alcohol. On a whim, she looked through the bottles, careful to not let anything clink and wake up Alberto or Richard. She was happy it was so late and that Richard was asleep, happy that it was still nighttime. The nights belonged to her. It was the only good thing about not sleeping much and not having a nine-to-five job.

Isabella spotted the almost-full bottle of Courvoisier. Richard hated cognac and had complained loudly when they'd bought the pricey bottle for her last birthday party. Looking at the bottle of amber liquid now, she felt conflicted. There'd been a few nights when she had stood right there, wanting a drink for some reason, but not able to indulge due to the breastfeeding.

Still, she'd always known that if she could have a drink, it would be a glass from this bottle, not because she was a big fan of cognac, but simply because Richard wasn't. It had felt like a form of rebellion, the thought of drinking something he abhorred. It had taken her right back to her childhood and her pointless little rebellions against her mother.

She wanted to rail against him, as one would against a strict parent. Or a jailer. And Richard was never supposed to be that. Richard would never want to be that.

She squeezed her eyes shut, as the realization of the truth hit her; he had never been her jailer—she had. She'd locked herself into this relationship, into this perfect showroom of a house, into this claustrophobic snob town, into this far too sunny state. She'd forced herself into a life, because it had seemed the right thing to do, for Alberto, for the rest of the world. It was what she was expected to do. And she'd pretended not to hate it. Now, she stood staring at the bottle of cognac and dreaming of a million tiny rebellions.

Isabella grabbed the bottle and held it tight. She was going to bring it upstairs. Not to drink from it. Alberto might wake up and need to be fed, and she was too tired to go through the hassle of pumping out milk before and calculating how many hours until the alcohol left her bloodstream.

No, she was bringing it up with her because she needed to look at it. She needed to remember the nights she was so eager to escape the prison of her own making that daydreaming of such a pointless rebellion had been her only escape. Well, the only escape she'd allowed herself. She had to remember that no matter how she tried to pretend everything was fine, her unhappiness was real. And more importantly, her unhappiness mattered.

She went upstairs and put the bottle of cognac down on the small table that held her iPad. The glass of the elegant bottle glittered in the dim glow of Alberto's night-light. She looked from the symbolic bottle to her sleeping son.

Alberto needed a father, but even if she left Florida and took him with her, he would still have Richard. As it was, they saw each other every night when Richard came home from work, but in fleeting moments. For all the interaction the two of them had, Richard seemed more like an uncle than a father.

She'd thought it was her fault. That she was the wedge between them. But was she? Really? Meeting Erin had made her question the assumption. Richard could have stood up to her. He could've made more of an effort. There'd been nothing to stop him from coming up to Alberto's nursery in the evenings. Nothing to stop him asking questions or taking time off to spend with Alberto.

Instead, Richard spent all his time off work with Joshua. She'd never questioned that, never even thought twice about that. After all, Richard couldn't see Joshua every day, so it made sense that he wanted to spend time with him when he could. But why hadn't he tried to combine the two things? He could always bring Joshua to the house to meet his little brother. She'd even suggested that a few times after Alberto was born, but Richard had said that he didn't want Joshua to feel jealous of Alberto.

Isabella stared at that bottle. Something had to change.

Her thoughts moved to Erin. She wouldn't leave Richard to be with Erin. It was too early to consider another relationship, no matter how tempting it was. This was a decision that would shape her life, as well as the lives of Alberto and Richard. It was much bigger than her infatuation with Erin. It had to be, otherwise she was making the decision for the wrong reason.

She took a few deep breaths, holding her hand on her stomach and feeling it move with each one.

Her choices were as clear as they'd always been. The stakes were just higher now. Now, she was aware of her unhappiness. Either she stayed for Alberto's sake, or she left for her own.

In the crib next to her, Alberto woke up with a cry. She was on her feet and picking him up in the blink of an eye. He barely cried after she picked him up, and Isabella wondered if he had woken due to a stomachache, some form of dream, or some odd premonition that she was considering leaving his father.

Then Alberto burped, and Isabella laughed. Clearly, there was no ominous foreboding about the breakup of his parents in Alberto's life, just a gassy stomach and the need to be picked up and loved. She looked at his little face as he yawned.

Could I love him even better if I were happy?

Chapter 19

Is It Too Much?

ERIN TRAINED HER CLIENTS WITH impressive vigor. Yesterday, she'd gone about her work diligently to ease her restlessness and stop her thoughts. Today, it was because she was full of a strange energy, halfway between positive and negative. But the combination had the same effect—Erin worked hard. Damn hard.

As she demonstrated moves, she had to remind herself not to push her clients as much as she was pushing herself. It got to the point where she was counting the number of repetitions for her current client and doing chest openers as well. Anything to keep moving.

When Erin got home, there was a note saying a delivery had been attempted for a package that needed a signature. Erin checked the clock on her phone. She had just enough time to get to the post office before they closed for the evening. She put her long boots back on and hurried out to the subway.

Finally, back home with her package and too tired to make dinner, she made turkey sandwiches and was about to make coffee, when she remembered that her package would have Isabella's fancy coffee in it. *Wonder if it will it go with turkey on rye? Only one way to find out.*

The neatly packed box was surprisingly big for a bag of coffee. When she used a pair of scissors to break into it, she understood why. There was a half-full bag of coffee, yes. But that wasn't all. There was something in a square box, wrapped in bubble wrap and, underneath it, a thick envelope.

Erin looked at the envelope. Isabella had said she would send her an account of how she met Richard and why she stayed with him. Well, something like that, anyway. She looked from the dreaded envelope to the mystery box and wondered which she should open first.

She decided on the box. The letter would be better focused on with a full stomach. Or maybe she was procrastinating, because the letter scared her. Just a bit.

She cut through the bubble wrap and looked at the smaller box. Beneath the heading *FitWatch 9000* was a picture of a guy jogging and, next to him, a close-up of one of those watches that was also a fitness tracker.

Erin felt thoroughly confused. Was there really a FitWatch in there, or had Isabella sent her some little thing and reused an old box? Surely, Isabella hadn't bought her something this expensive? Those things were more than a hundred bucks.

Erin opened the box and looked down at a square, digital watch with pulse monitor and the whole shebang. Yep, Isabella had sent her the actual fitness watch.

Could it be a mistake somehow? Then she remembered that she'd told Isabella about her ruined watch and that she wasn't planning to buy a new one until she got paid. Clearly, Isabella had wanted to fix the problem.

Erin gave a low whistle. This "fix" was advanced and awesome. She'd have to double-check with Isabella that she hadn't paid an arm and a leg for it. If it seemed like she'd paid more than she could comfortably afford, Erin was sending it back. If Isabella was as well off as her previous work title and fancy house suggested, well then, Erin wasn't too proud to keep the gift. *After all, it's not like I've gotten a lot of gifts in my life. I need to learn to accept them at some point. Might as well start now.*

Erin looked at the envelope again, biting her lip, and remembered she was supposed to be eating. She got the coffee grounds and introduced her coffee maker to the most exotic thing it had ever contained. She had to admit the grounds smelled nice, like the burnt sugar they'd apparently been stored with.

When the coffee was done, Erin sat down, her rye sandwiches brimming with avocado, romaine lettuce, and turkey. She ate quickly, too curious to take her time. But she took the time to savor the coffee; it was so good. So damn good. She didn't think she could taste the burnt sugar in the flavor, but it tasted nutty and of something rich that she couldn't put her finger on. Either way, it was good enough for Erin to decide to try and invest in some more when she ran out of this bag.

When she finished the sandwiches, she shoved the plate away and put the half-empty coffee cup to the side. She wanted—no, she needed—to read what Isabella had written.

Erin read thoroughly and had to admit it felt a bit like she was reading a book. She made a mental note to let Isabella know; surely a writer would appreciate hearing something like that? The whole thing was three pages long. At the bottom of the last page, for some unknown reason, Isabella had closed with her signature.

Erin, still lost in thought from all she had read, looked at the name, *Isabella Martinez*, was written in neat, slightly slanted handwriting.

She couldn't stop staring. She traced the signature with her fingers, knowing that it had been less than forty-eight hours since Isabella's fingers had been so close to the paper Erin was now touching. The compulsion was stupid, of course, Isabella had handled the entire package. If Erin wanted to feel close to the other woman's touch, she should just touch the objects themselves, as Isabella must have handled them. Still, there was an inexplicable intimacy in touching Isabella's signature, as if it was part of Isabella herself.

The letter made Erin understand more about that odd relationship between her and Richard. It made a lot more sense now.

It also made sense that Isabella had to leave him. She didn't love him and didn't really want to be living in Florida with him. Alberto wasn't going to benefit from having a mom who was unhappy and closing herself off from people—and, worse, closing herself off from her own feelings.

What Erin couldn't decide was what would happen between herself and Isabella. It wasn't like Isabella would move to New York; they hadn't even met, for Pete's sake. Isabella might stay in Florida so Alberto could be close to Richard, or she might go back to Philadelphia.

Well, Philly wasn't that far away from New York, and her misery lifted a little. But even if she could see Isabella and they had a chance for a future, she knew nothing about babies. She closed her eyes and rubbed her forehead. *How would I handle Alberto? I'm not exactly mother material, am I?*

Erin Black, the notorious lone wolf? Would that really fit in with Isabella and her family, and her baby groups?

It was such a huge leap to go from realizing that, yes, she had a crush on a woman she met online, to considering if she could ever meet said woman and form a relationship with her…and her baby. Perhaps, she was being selfish to even think about her own role in this when Isabella had such big decisions to make.

It was too much. Erin held her hands up and decided to focus on what she knew for sure; she'd fallen in love with Isabella Martinez, and she wanted Isabella to be happy.

She looked over at her new watch and beamed. She had to thank Isabella and make sure that she could afford to be splashing out on her like this. And she had to make sure of that before she ripped the thing open and started playing with it. Oh, and yes, they most certainly had to talk about that letter.

Erin booted up her laptop, and the second it was on, she clicked into Skype.

> **BlackVelvetBitches:** Hey, Ms. Writer. You online?

She sat back and stared at the screen, hoping.

> **IsabellaMartinez1:** Briefly, yes. I'm making dinner so I'll have to put the iPad away soon.

> **BlackVelvetBitches:** Okay. First of all: Thank you SO MUCH for the package! I've tried the coffee and read the letter and lost my shit over the FitWatch :-D

> **IsabellaMartinez1:** I'm so glad to hear it arrived in good condition and that you liked it. Richard will be home any second, so I should hurry up with dinner, but perhaps we can speak later? I can convince Richard to take Alberto for an evening walk and we can perhaps video call? I think we might need to talk about the letter face-to-face.

Erin shouted, "Hell yes," probably annoying the neighbor again. She was going to see Isabella again, and maybe they could finally get some answers before this thing ate her whole from the inside. She calmed herself enough to type.

> **BlackVelvetBitches:** Sure. One thing before I let you go, though? Are you sure about this watch thingy? It must have cost you a fortune?

> **IsabellaMartinez1:** I can easily afford it. Consider it payment for your stretching instructions and the refresher course I'm sure I'll need soon. Enjoy it, and let me know if it is any good.

Erin could live with that.

> **BlackVelvetBitches:** I'm sure it's going to be awesome. Thank you so freakin' much, Isabella!

> **IsabellaMartinez1:** You're welcome, preciosa. I'd better get back to dinner before it burns to a crisp. Speak soon.

> **BlackVelvetBitches:** Yeah, catch you later!

A rush of happiness hit again, as Erin looked at the square box containing her new treasure. Unexpectedly, her Skype pinged with a new message.

> **IsabellaMartinez1:** To make sure we can easily reach each other even when we are not online, why don't I give you my phone number so you can text me? And vice versa, if I need to get hold of you?

> **BlackVelvetBitches:** Great idea!

Erin wrote out her number and Isabella replied with hers.

> **IsabellaMartinez1:** There, I have that in my BlackBerry now. I'll speak to you after we've eaten.

> **BlackVelvetBitches:** Cool, I'll mock you for having a Blackberry later then. :-P Enjoy dinner, and kiss the kid on his fluffy little head for me.

Erin wasn't sure if she was assuming too much, but she felt pretty sure that there was a woman in Naples, Florida looking at the words *his fluffy little head* her iPad screen and rolling her eyes. It was way too much fun to tease Isabella about her cute lil' man.

Chapter 20

One Step Ahead

ISABELLA PUT ALBERTO IN HIS baby bouncer by her chair and quickly grabbed her iPad. She knew she'd made Erin wait for far too long, but there had been no other choice.

She clicked the button to call Erin and got a reply quickly. The screen resolved into the image of the blonde New Yorker, this time with her hair down and resting against her T-shirt clad shoulders. Isabella knitted her brows.

"Aren't you cold, Erin? You're in a T-shirt!"

"No, I'm actually a bit sweaty. I've been doing jumping jacks with my new FitWatch on and monitoring my pulse. This thing is great! Thank you, again."

"Don't mention it. I'm glad you are enjoying it."

The smile on the screen faded, and Erin looked right into the camera before speaking again. "And the coffee was yummy, so thanks for that too."

"It is very nice, isn't it? Unique flavor, I think. I've ordered three more packages. They should be arriving any day now."

"Good idea. It's delicious. But I suppose, we should talk about the letter, right?"

Isabella's pulse rate suddenly climbed to heights that Erin's FitWatch would probably be impressed with. She knew she should actually be talking about what had made her keep Erin waiting for so long. But as it was connected to the contents of the letter, and as she didn't know where to start, this was as good a place as any.

"Yes, I suppose we should. So, what were your thoughts?" Isabella asked.

With a heavy sigh, Erin spoke. "Well, first of all, I think it's admirable that you tried to make a family for Alberto, even though you didn't know Richard or have much in common with him. Secondly, I know how easily you can be fooled into thinking that someone is right for you, just because they gave you what you needed at a certain point of your life. I've had relationships like that in the past."

"Right. You understand what happened. I'm glad to hear it," Isabella said.

Erin was fidgeting in her seat. It looked like she was steeling herself. Isabella braced herself for what might come next.

"I have to be honest, though. I don't think it's a good enough reason for you to stay with him. I'm not just saying that because of how I feel about you. I'm not in this equation. I can't be. It's just that you are too amazing to force yourself to live a life you feel trapped in. Alberto's not going to thank you for making him grow up in a pretend family, you know? Remember the stuff I said after you had that nightmare? All that still stands. Anyway, it's not really any of my business, but it breaks my heart to think of you being as unhappy as you seem in this letter."

Isabella smiled a little to herself. Erin didn't know, of course, what had happened before this call, just after she and Richard ate dinner. Erin hadn't been there to see the walls come tumbling down. It was so strange. Isabella had had serious conversations in the past. But all she remembered, even right after they'd taken place, was a blur of fearful emotions followed either by relief when the conversation ended positively, or dread and defeat when it ended badly.

Tonight's conversation was different. This one she remembered in minute detail. It was as if her fear and anxiety had heightened her presence in the moment and seared it into her mind. She could recall the scent of their dinner still lingering in the air, her clammy palms, and the look of unease on Richard's face. And every single word they'd said.

She hadn't planned to talk to him then. The idea had been to talk to Erin and see what an outsider thought. Then, probably, Isabella would have dedicated the following night to getting a babysitter and sitting down with

Richard, to spending the night explaining everything and building up to the big decision. Things were rarely that easy. Plans never seemed to work out in real life.

Instead, Isabella had looked at Richard, really looked at him, while they ate. He avoided her gaze. More than that, he avoided looking at Alberto, who sat in his baby bouncer next to the dining table, gumming at a toy.

There were dark rings under his eyes, and the furrows on his forehead had deepened substantially since she'd last looked at them. This was not a happy man. Isabella immediately gave up the thought that this was the life Richard wanted. He wasn't as complacent and satisfied with things as he'd seemed.

She put her knife and fork down on her plate. In the silent room, it clattered far too loudly. Richard glanced up and swallowed his mouthful. She placed her hand on top of his, and he looked at her, worry etched in every line of his face.

"Richard, are you all right?"

He hesitated before answering, and the smile on his face was painted on. "Yes, of course. I'm fit as a fiddle, and work's good. As usual."

She sighed. Couldn't he sense that she was beyond their usual game of pretense? "Be that as it may. I can tell that something is wrong," she prompted.

He cleared his throat. "There's...a lot on my mind."

Isabella removed her hand and sat back in her chair. "Well, if everything at work is good, I assume that the things on your mind concern our home life."

He looked as if he was about to deny it, but his face fell and he reached for his beer. He took a big gulp, then put the glass down. "Perhaps, yes. You can't fault me for that. I know something's eating you too, Isabella. You just aren't talking about it."

Her body started to give confusing signals. Her hands felt cold but sweaty, while her face felt flushed with heat. It was as if the words came from someone else. "Then let's change that. We need to talk about us."

He nodded and looked like a little boy about to get chastised by his parents.

She pressed on. She intertwined her fingers in her lap and held on to herself as though she could be comforted by holding her own hand.

"I don't know where to start this conversation. I was hoping to have a little more time to think this through but...here we are. So, I'll just say it. I wanted us to stay together to be good parents to Alberto, but I'm not happy. I haven't been since we decided to live together. That seemed like a fair trade before, but now...I've spoken to someone online who has made me realize what a different person I can be when I feel challenged and, well, contented, maybe. I think I could be a better mother, a better writer, and a better person if I was happy."

"I know," Richard said quietly.

Isabella stared up at him. Of all the things she had expected him to say to that admission, this was not one of them. "Excuse me?"

"I know. I've known for some time that you were miserable. I am too. I love you, Isabella, but we don't make a good couple. There's no passion, and we're so...out of sync. We don't have much to talk about, and we're always walking on eggshells around each other. Sometimes, God, sometimes, it feels like you're a stranger!"

Isabella felt the heat in her face increase, and she started to feel dizzy. "Then...why haven't you said anything?"

"The same reason as you. I wanted us to be a family for Alberto, and I wasn't sure if I deserved to be selfish here. I already failed as a husband and father once. I didn't want to fail again."

Isabella swallowed hard. "What's made you change your mind, then?"

Richard laughed but there was no joy in it. "Shay, funnily enough. About two weeks ago, when I went to pick up Joshua, she and I got to talking. Since then, we've spoken a few times a week. Just short calls on my lunch break, nothing shady."

He paused and looked almost wistful as he continued, "But she says she misses me, she said she misses her best friend. Can you imagine that, Isabella? Being married to your best friend? There's nothing quite like it. I guess being separated has made us both realize that. I've been thinking about it ever since. I don't know what to do."

Isabella tried to take a deep breath but only sucked in a little air in a quick hiss, as if her lungs refused to open properly until this was all resolved.

"You mean you're considering going back to Shay and Joshua?"

Richard frowned and scratched his head agitatedly. "I don't know. I feel bad, like having a new family made me realize how much I loved my old one. But it's not like that. You and Alberto mean a lot to me, and I will always adore Alberto. It's just…"

"Your heart lies elsewhere," Isabella suggested softly.

"Yes, exactly. I don't want to walk out on you and Alberto, though. I promised I wouldn't do that. I can't go back on that now, no matter what I'm feeling. After all, it's because of me that you are living in Florida, and I know you quit your job in Philadelphia, giving up your income. But…I just…feel like I'm letting you down all the time. I don't want to keep doing that. However, I don't want to break my promise about staying either."

"You won't be." Isabella smiled softly. "Not if we're both setting ourselves free from a loveless relationship to go in search of what makes us happy. Don't worry about my financial situation. I have savings, as you know, and the family fortune to fall back on, if I really need it. Besides, when Alberto is older, I was going to try to find work again, anyway."

There was a long, heavy pause.

"So, what are you going to do, Isabella? Are you moving back to Philadelphia?"

Isabella sighed. "I don't know. I'm not sure I want to take Alberto so far away from you."

Richard turned to look at Alberto, who was shaking his toy animatedly and then putting it back into his mouth.

"Well, right now, I live under the same roof as him, and I barely see him. When I'm home, he's always with you, up in that room. I don't see him on weekends, and he doesn't even sleep in the same room as me. He barely knows who I am. Part of that is that you are so close to him, and part of it is that I feel so disconnected from him. He never felt like my son. Maybe that's because we never felt like a family. And that's on me. I should've made more of an effort."

He stopped for a moment. Isabella watched him swallow visibly and grip onto the table with whitening knuckles. He looked like he needed the support of the sturdy, wooden table to be able to get the next words out. "But lately, I've felt guilty when I look at him. Guilty because I haven't spent time with him. And if I'm honest, guilty because Joshua feels more like my son than he does. Isn't that despicable? I'm such a shitty father."

Isabella pressed her lips together and shook her head. The honesty of the conversation was making her uncomfortable, but she forced herself to stay put and keep talking.

"It isn't just your fault. I kept Alberto to myself, because I didn't trust anyone else, and maybe because on some level...I didn't want him to love anyone but me. Because if he did, he might prefer them to me. And I don't know if I could survive that."

Richard tried to hide a sniffle, but Isabella could see he was crying.

"Anyway, things are the way they are. If I were to see him less often, it would force me to make the effort, and you'd have to let go a little if he was going to have any relationship with me at all. I think it would force us both to alter the behavior that got us into this mess as parents."

"I would let go more then, yes. As you say, I'd have to if I didn't want him to lose out on having a connection with you. If I moved back to Philadelphia and you moved in with Shay and Joshua, I suppose you would spend your weekdays with Joshua, freeing your weekends and vacations up to visit Alberto? And when Alberto gets older, he and I can come down here to visit."

Richard sniffed, and Isabella handed him her unused napkin. He thanked her and blew his nose. "Yeah, I suppose. You know that I've always loved traveling, and going up to Philly to see my boy could be a nice tradition. I mean, who knows? I might not live in Florida for the rest of my life. There are plenty of nature reserves in this country that could use me fighting for them," he said with hope in his voice.

Isabella hoped her smile showed the tenderness she felt. "Of course. And maybe Alberto and I will miss the Florida sun and come back one day. Whatever happens, I won't let my son grow up completely without a father. I'll bend over backward to ensure you two spend time together, be that face-to-face whenever we have time or via Skype calls."

Richard smiled back. "Either way, the time I spend with him might not be in huge quantity, but we'll damn well make sure it's higher in quality than what he has now."

Isabella's eyes stung with tears, but she kept smiling.

All of a sudden, Richard chuckled, making her jump.

"Sorry, I didn't mean to startle you. It's just...whoa. What a relief. I can't believe months of complacency and weeks of agonizing was resolved so damn fast!"

Isabella laughed too, trying not to blink so the tears wouldn't fall. "Yes, we're lucky that we were *both* unhappy and questioning things. I suppose we were finally in sync for the last leg of our relationship. Better late than never."

"I suppose so," Richard said.

They were quiet for a while, both getting their bearings. Richard drank deep from his beer, and Isabella slowly released her intertwined fingers, which had gone numb from the squeezing. She brushed away a single tear that escaped her eye and wiped underneath it to clean off any mascara. She wouldn't cry. If she did, she'd break down completely. And that was not the way Isabella Martinez had been raised. As always, she heard her mother's voice. *Losing control over yourself is losing in life, Isabella.*

It was Richard who finally broke the long silence. "So, um, are you going to tell me about him?"

"Who? Alberto?"

"No, the guy! The guy you met online, the one who made you realize that you were unhappy."

Isabella hummed, feeling the corners of her mouth quirk up. "Remember that evening when I told you I was going to go upstairs and talk to a woman in New York?"

"Uh, yeah, vague memory of that, yes. Hang on, was she the chick who showed you stretches or something while I took care of Alberto on Sunday?"

Isabella braced herself. "Yes, that's Erin. Well, she's 'the guy.'"

Richard looked confused. "Oh, right. Sorry, I thought it was someone who was romantically interested in you that made you face up to your unhappiness."

"It was. She is interested in me, and the feeling is mutual, even though it is still very early days. However, I hasten to add that I am not going to jump into a relationship with her. She isn't the reason I believe we should end our relationship."

"No, I get that. Our breakup is about you and me, not about this woman you met or about Shay. I have to say, though, I didn't know you were..."

"Bisexual? Neither did I, really. If that is what I am. All I know is that I am interested in her, and she's made me feel things I haven't felt for a very long time. If ever. Maybe one day, something will come of it. But for now, I'm just grateful that her appearance in my life opened my eyes, for all our sakes—yours, mine, and most importantly, Alberto's."

After that, there hadn't been much to say. They both had plans to iron out, decisions to make, and people to talk to about their conversation.

When Isabella's hand fell onto his shoulder, she felt how warm it was from all his anxious energy. He had looked up at her with grateful, tear-filled eyes when she told him he should go call Shay. She took over his usual job of washing the dishes.

When she was finished, she'd grabbed Alberto and climbed the stairs to talk to Erin. Now, here she was, listening to Erin carefully trying to prompt her to have the life-shattering conversation that she'd just had. She realized she was grinning.

Erin did too. "Why are you smiling like that? Are you okay?"

"Yes, Erin. I'm fine. I'm smiling because I am one step ahead of you."

She told Erin everything and was met by stunned silence at first.

"Well, fuck me," Erin said.

Chapter 21

Figuring Out the Next Step

ERIN DIDN'T KNOW WHAT TO say about Isabella and Richard's decision. She tried to keep the obvious relief off her face, out of respect for Isabella and what she must be going through.

"That was really brave. It can't have been easy," she said sincerely.

Isabella gave a laugh that sounded more like a scoff. "No. It certainly wasn't. I'm glad it's done, though."

There was a noise, and Erin saw Isabella look down to the floor.

"Hang on, Alberto's starting to fidget. I think he wants to come up," Isabella said.

She placed the iPad on some form of stand on the table and then reached out of view. When she came back up, she had Alberto in her arms. He was wearing what looked like tiny baby jeans and a dark blue sweater that matched Isabella's dress perfectly.

Erin looked back up to Isabella's face and grinned. "Hey, Martinez...?"

Isabella looked up.

She felt her smile grow bigger. "Did you and the lil' man color-coordinate this morning?"

Isabella looked confused. She looked down at her own outfit and Alberto's. When her gaze returned upward, her lips were pursed. "That was a coincidence, Erin. I do not dress him to match my outfit. He's not an accessory."

"Whatever you say. You both look good in blue, though."

Isabella smiled a little. "Thank you." She looked down at the baby, lying in her arms and yawning. "Alberto. Say thank you to the nice lady." Alberto didn't make a noise, so his mother prompted him by tickling him. He squirmed and gave a giggling squeak.

"Was that supposed to be a 'thank you?'" Erin asked through her laughter.

Isabella raised her eyebrows. "Excuse me. Just the other day you were saying I shouldn't be so hard on his lack of conversation skills and that he's trying his best."

"You're right!" Erin held up her hands. "I'll take the weird giggle noise as a sign of gratitude." She looked from Isabella's face down to the baby in her arms. "You're welcome, kid."

Alberto kicked his feet a little, stopped, and held very still for a second, then burped loudly. It was a sound that couldn't have come from such a small body.

Erin laughed so hard she almost fell out of the chair. She looked up to see Isabella just barely hiding a smile. When Erin's laughter died out, Isabella looked down at Alberto and said, "That wasn't very nice, *mi vida*."

Alberto didn't reply. He just lay there and looked up at her. Erin was looking at Isabella too, with two warring emotions buzzing around her head. The first was that Isabella was so lovely when she was being tender with her son, and the other one was about how sexy it was when Isabella spoke Spanish, even just a couple of words.

But she was determined to keep her mouth shut on both subjects. Isabella was just barely single, and Erin didn't want to take advantage of the situation. So she just sat there, smiling at her and enjoying watching her beam down at Alberto and stroke the baby's hair.

In the end, though, Erin had to end the comfortable silence. "So, um, we have a while to talk before he needs to sleep, right?"

"Yes, we have some time. He needs a bath tonight, but there's no hurry."

Erin froze at the look of those intense eyes meeting hers. "Right. So, um, should we talk about what happens next? Or do you want to wait with that?" Erin felt an uneasy sensation in the pit of her stomach. Was she pushing this too much and too quickly?

"We can talk about it. Just don't expect me to make any big decisions right now. I've had a bit of a stressful evening."

"No! No, of course not. I just wanted to tell you that I don't have any expectations. About you and me, I mean. You are just starting the process of a breakup, and you have to focus on yourself and Alberto. I wanted you to know that I understand. I won't try to worm my way into anything, as long as you know that I'm here for you and that you can talk to me, and not just as someone who has a crush on you but as a friend. Breakups suck, and I want to be here for you."

"Thank you. That means a lot to me. I think what I'll mainly need from you is distraction. Talking to you makes me happy. And I'll probably need a lot of that through this process."

Erin bit her lip around her own smile. "That sounds like an awesome job. I accept the position. I'll be your, um, what is it called—the clown guy who entertained old kings?"

Isabella furrowed her brow. "The court jester?"

"That's the one! I'll be your court jester."

"I believe court jesters were meant to look silly and comical, not as breathtaking as you are."

Erin stopped dead and stared at Isabella openmouthed. She hadn't expected a huge compliment and a clear flirtation like that. She didn't know what to answer.

Isabella adjusted her grip on Alberto, moving him up to her shoulder and patting his back. But her eyes were on Erin. Her smile looked playful. "Close your mouth, beautiful. You'll catch flies."

Erin clamped her jaw shut and tried to hide what was probably a goofy smile while tucking some hair behind her ear. The evening was just getting better and better.

"Anyway, back to what you were saying. I'm glad you are not expecting me to jump straight into a relationship right away, and a long-distance one at that. Both for my sake and yours. This is not just because I am emotionally unstable right now, nor because we have only known each other for a short while, but because you deserve better than being my rebound relationship." Her smile was replaced with a look of tenderness and solemnity.

Erin nodded with an earnestness she hoped showed on Isabella's little iPad screen. Alberto was fussing at Isabella's shoulder, and it looked to Erin like he was trying to bite her.

"He's looking for food," she explained. "I'll have to rearrange the order of things tonight. I'll feed him and then give him his bath. Would you mind hanging up? I can't reach the iPad."

Erin didn't want to end the call. She would happily sit there and watch Isabella give Alberto his baby bottle for hours on end, anything to get more of Isabella and her cute little kid.

Dreamily, she said, "Why don't you go ahead and feed him? I don't mind. I just like your company."

Isabella looked right at the camera with an incredulous look. Erin wondered what that meant and frowned deeply.

"What? I don't mind if you can't talk while you feed him," Erin said in confusion.

"That's not what concerns me, Miss Black. It's the fact that I have to take this dress halfway off. Not to mention unclasp my bra and then...well... I'm not sure you should see what is inside that particular garment just yet."

Erin felt like her world was in the middle of an earthquake. Shit! What did she just say? She hadn't considered that Isabella breastfed the kid.

"Oh my God! Isabella, I'm so freakin' sorry. I thought you were going to feed him with a bottle. I mean, I am all for the desexualizing of breastfeeding, but I didn't mean to sound like I was pushing for you to take your dress off in front of me or something. Fuck, I'm such an idiot!"

Isabella laughed, and it seemed to come all the way from her toes. It was a deep, musical laugh that made Erin all warm and fuzzy. This was how she wanted to make Isabella laugh, without any inhibitions or concern. *Shame I had to make a complete ass of myself to do it.*

When she'd recovered from her fit of laughter, Isabella smiled at her. "Don't worry. I assumed there'd been some form of miscommunication. Hopefully one day, I'll get to undress in front of you for more interesting reasons than feeding Alberto. For now, I think I'm going to go put my pajamas on and then feed him before he eats my collarbone."

"Okay, I'll hang up the call. Uh, but before you go, I have to say it again... Isabella, I'm so sorry."

Isabella adjusted the fussing baby and looked back to Erin. "For what? My breakup or suggesting I strip on camera?"

"I-I...I didn't..." Erin stammered, tripping over her own tongue.

Something like pity appeared in her eyes. "I'm sorry, I'm just toying with you now. It's far too much fun, and you are impossibly cute when you blush, Miss Black. No need to apologize. I'll try for some sleep tonight, I think. So I won't be back later. Want to Skype tomorrow night?"

"Of course! Text chat at midnight, or video call before Alberto's bedtime again?"

Isabella smirked. "I suppose that depends on if you want to see me again or if you just want to talk."

"I think you know I want both. Really, really want both," Erin said before swallowing hard.

Why do I feel so nervous now? It's not like I'm inviting her on some kind of date.

"Me too. Seeing you is quite addictive, Erin. Just as addictive as chatting to you has been since that first night, actually. I'll video call you tomorrow then? About nine thirty?"

"I'll be here with bells on," Erin said enthusiastically.

"Now that sounds like an interesting sight. Good night, *preciosa*. I hope you can sleep."

"Same to you. Oh, and Isabella, text or call me on my phone if you need to talk tonight. Anytime you need me, I'll be here. I mean that."

"Thank you so much." Alberto started crying, and Isabella hushed and rocked him. "I better go feed him before he gets angry. I'm afraid he's inherited my temper."

"Well, that serves you right, Martinez. Now, go get that dress off and feed the kid!"

It wasn't until she had said it that she started worrying about ordering Isabella to take her clothes off, even for innocent reasons. She bit her tongue, cursing it for all the dumb stuff it always said.

Mercifully, Isabella was too busy with Alberto to stop and tease her about the remark. She just gave her a quirked eyebrow and walked out of the room.

As she watched her leave, Erin realized that she was probably going to her bedroom to get changed. She closed her eyes and forced her lovesick brain not to think about Isabella undressing.

With one last look at the empty chair where Isabella would no doubt spend the night, Erin sighed and ended the call. It shocked her how completely she had fallen. No matter how slowly Isabella needed to take it, Erin hoped that deep down, Isabella felt the same way.

Chapter 22

Bookshops and Backs

ISABELLA, AND A SOUNDLY SLEEPING Alberto, had driven to the nearest shopping mall after breakfast. Isabella's mind was swimming with all the changes that were coming her way, so she had to get out of the house for a while. She had to let everything digest in her mind. After some pacing in the kitchen, she had decided to go somewhere that always calmed her, a bookstore.

With Alberto cozy in his stroller, she wandered the aisles, looking at the book covers and spines. Just for a moment, she dared to daydream about seeing her name on a book on one of those shelves.

She picked up a Kate Atkinson book but then reminded herself that while she loved to buy and own books, she didn't have much time to read lately. She shouldn't waste money or accrue more belongings, now that she was going to move out. It only meant more to pack, more to haul, and more to store.

Her phone vibrated in her handbag, almost waking Alberto. She quickly retrieved the phone and groaned when she saw that it was Judith calling.

"Hello, Mother."

"Isabella? Where are you? I can hear people in the background."

"Alberto and I are in a bookstore. We needed a little excursion."

Judith scoffed. "You brought him with you? I cannot for the life of me understand why you are so glued to that child. It's not good for him, Isabella. He's going to grow up to be far too dependent on you. Even worse, he's going to assume that everyone in his life is going to dote on him. Just you wait and see. He'll be crying for his mother at every hurdle. You are stifling the boy."

Isabella stopped walking and closed her eyes for a moment. "Am I to assume this is heading toward the nanny argument again?"

"Yes, actually. Having a nanny would solve two problems. It would break his dependency on you, and you could return to work, ensuring that at least one of his parents has a proper career. And brings in the sort of money that will send Alberto to Harvard."

The last sentence had been said under her mother's breath, but it was still perfectly audible. Judith Martinez didn't say anything she didn't want the world to hear.

"I have made financial arrangements for Alberto's future. You don't need to worry about that," Isabella muttered.

"But I do worry, Isabella. I worry that in your refusal to listen to someone who has been in your situation, you are damaging your son. It's not healthy to take him everywhere with you."

Isabella wanted to argue with that. She wanted to bring up all the times she felt abandoned when she grew up. All the times when her mother should have been there. School plays. Marie breaking her arm. Isabella's first breakup with a boy. But Judith was busy working, playing golf, going to art exhibitions, gossiping with her acquaintances from different charity boards, or getting a manicure—anything that didn't involve Isabella or Marie.

Her shoulders slumped, as she played out the flip side of her mother's arguments. Maybe she was too clingy with Alberto. She was well aware of that possibility and trying to work on it. But there had to be a balance between her own clinginess and the borderline neglect she and Marie had grown up with.

Deep down, she was terrified that her mother was right. Maybe she was damaging Alberto. Maybe she was raising him incorrectly, and he would be scarred.

Always that nagging fear of not being good enough.

With that in mind, Isabella merely replied, "I know you worry. I'll take your advice under consideration."

It was deeply unsatisfying, and she ached to fight back. But sometimes you had to take the easy way out. *Pick your battles. You still have to tell her about leaving Richard, and heaven knows how she's going to take that.*

"Was there a reason for your call, Mother? Because if there wasn't, I might take this opportunity to tell you about a recent development."

"No other reason than to check in. I hadn't heard from you in quite a while."

And there was the guilt trip for not calling. Isabella grimaced. Her mother was in good form today.

"I see. Well, then I should tell you that Richard and I have decided to go our separate ways."

There was a long beat of silence.

"Separate ways? As in terminating your relationship?"

"Yes," Isabella replied tiredly.

"Permanently?"

"Yes."

"Well, I am glad to hear that you have come to your senses."

The smug tone in her mother's voice made Isabella feel sick. She wanted to punch something. She opened her eyes and made sure no one could see the look that was no doubt plastered on her face.

Isabella cleared her throat to get her voice under control. "I really don't need to hear that. Just be happy that you don't have to worry about Richard anymore. Oh, and if you are even thinking about saying "I told you so," rest assured that I *will* hang up on you."

"Fine. I won't say it. May I at least ask what will happen with my grandson?"

"Of course you can. He will stay with me when I move out. Richard will visit as much as he can, and we will visit him as well."

"I see. You and Alberto are moving out and *he* isn't?"

Isabella tried to ignore the tone of voice.

"I'm not sure. We still have to decide whether we are going to sell the house, or if Richard wants to stay living there. After all, he loves that house, while I'm not particularly attached to it. The location is very convenient for his job. Besides, he's probably reuniting with his ex-wife and older son. If he does, they'll need a big house."

"A-ha! He cheated on you with his ex-wife, and that is why you finally came to your senses and left him."

Isabella felt the niggling tension of an impending headache between her eyes. She was clenching her jaw so tightly that her teeth were beginning to ache. "No, Mother. That's not why."

"But *you* are leaving *him*?"

"We decided to leave each other. Our relationship wasn't working. It was based on trying to do the right thing for Alberto, rather than on being in love with each other."

Judith scoffed. "And he is moving in with his ex-wife right away? Sounds like he is simply replacing you and Alberto."

"Mother, don't judge when you don't know the facts. He has his motives, and I have mine. In the end, it all boils down to the fact that we were trying to force ourselves to live a lie. Yesterday, we decided to put an end to that and move on. Can we change the topic now? I'm sure you have another hundred questions lined up."

Her mother sniffed, clearly faking nonchalance. "So, you are moving out of the house. Where to? Are you going to stay down there with the retirees, holidaymakers, and alligators?"

She gritted her teeth before answering, "I don't plan to stay in Florida, no."

"Good. You know how frizzy the humidity makes your hair."

Isabella bristled at the comment. But she wasn't surprised.

Yes, of course. My looks are what's important here. Have to look perfect and act perfect, never mind being happy. That's not the Martinez way.

It was amazing how her mother's judgment could make her want to defend something. "Cold and wet weather is almost worse for that, Mother. Florida is humid, but it's not the biggest culprit when it comes to frizz."

"Be that as it may, it's not doing your hair any favors."

"I suppose not," Isabella muttered grudgingly.

"If you move back to Philadelphia, you will be making your father ecstatically happy. He has been so bored lately. I have my work, the country club, and my charities. But your father does nothing but sit and read in that dusty, old office. Oh, and gossip with his friends over fatty treats. It'll do him good to see you and Alberto a few times a week."

Isabella took a deep breath. She had been considering where to move when she left Florida. Philadelphia was a good choice. She knew it like the back of her hand and really liked the city in general. Not too big, not too small. It also came with the added bonus of seeing her beloved father more. And she had to admit that Philadelphia would be convenient if she needed work. She could always try to get back into her old company.

There's another point in the pro column, isn't there? It's not too far away from New York, right?

She shook the last thought away. Erin wasn't supposed to be in the picture. At least not yet. And, anyway, Philadelphia had one serious downside. The person she was speaking to right now.

"Well? Are you coming back home?"

"I don't know, Mother. This has just happened. Nothing has been decided yet."

"There's no time like the present, you know," Judith said in a voice laced with impatience.

Isabella ran her hand over her face, making sure not to touch her eyes and ruin her makeup. She collected herself as best she could before answering.

"My whole life is changing at breakneck speed. I'll need a few days to get my bearings. Do you think you can you wait a few days?"

"No need to be facetious. Of course I can wait. Just don't let too much time pass. The house market moves fast."

"Yes, Mother."

Isabella noticed that she was in the way of another customer and began to walk slowly down the aisle. She had to find a way to end this call with minimum drama.

Her mother's speaking pace upped, showing that she was irate about something. "Did I tell you that our neighbors put their house up for sale last week? They think they already have a buyer. And they put that house up for much more than market value, I'll have you know."

Isabella merely hummed as a reply, too exhausted with this conversation to add words. Her eyes wandered back to the book covers, as her mother carried on talking about the neighbors and what they had sold their house for.

A book caught her eye. She had reached the shop's nonfiction area, and the book in front of her bore the title *Women in Comics—A History.* Isabella parked the stroller to the side and picked up the book. The blurb informed her that it was a close look at both female characters in comics and the women who drew and wrote the stories. It was so interesting that Isabella missed far too much of her mother's diatribe and was caught out when her mother suddenly said, "Wouldn't you agree?"

She panicked for a moment, then decided that agreeing was usually the safest bet with her mother anyway. She just hoped that she wasn't about to condone her mother killing some poor family who did nothing more than get a good deal on their house.

"Yes, I absolutely agree."

"I thought you might, dear. People are intolerable."

"Yes, they are," Isabella agreed distractedly.

She was looking at the book. Hearing Erin talk about her reading habits had made her curious about the world of comics. That and how much she had enjoyed the latest Captain America movie. Although, if she were honest, that might have had more to do with Chris Evans...and, she realized, Scarlett Johansson. How had she not picked up on her interest in women until now?

Isabella froze for a second. It was uncomfortable talking to her mother while thinking about sexy women and her interest in them.

"Mother, I need to go. I'm almost by the cash register, and I have to pay. Can I call you later?"

"Well, yes, I suppose so. I should probably go make sure your father has remembered to take his vitamins today, anyway."

"Great. I'll call you later, then. Goodbye."

She hung up and put the phone back in her bag.

The book was still in her hand. She knew she was buying it, but what she was pondering now was whether she should buy a copy for Erin. It was just released, so she was fairly confident Erin wouldn't have it already.

She tapped her fingers against the book. Should she really buy Erin more gifts? What if Erin thought she was trying to buy her affection? Or if she started to feel like a charity case? Or, worse, what if she started seeing her as some sort of—what was the expression, *sugar mama*?

Isabella rolled her eyes at herself. Another book browser came barreling past her, and Isabella hurried out of his way. She felt her back twinge a little at the quick movement and found the perfect solution.

If she asked Erin for another personal trainer demonstration on back stretches, she could then send her the book as a thank-you. Perfectly natural and platonic. And with the added bonus of having an excuse to watch Erin stretch again.

Isabella temporarily put the book down and got her phone out again. She sent off a text to Erin.

> *Good morning. I know I'm talking to you on Skype tonight, but I wanted to ask if we could change the chat to another back-stretch session? I just felt a worrying twinge and want to repair the damage before my back gets worse.*

She tucked away the phone again and picked up two copies of the book before heading to the register. As she was paying, she heard her phone beep. She finished the transaction and left the shop, grabbing her phone as soon as she was outside.

> *Hey you! Abso-frickin-lutely. Get your exercise gear out tonight, and be prepared to stretch until you're as supple as a cat in the sun. Or something else that's really supple. I dunno. Xoxo*

Isabella smiled at the text. Staying single would be so much easier if Erin didn't make her this happy and lovesick just with a simple text.

Isabella was probably as ready as she was ever going to be, but she still ran over the checklist in her head. She was set up downstairs, in front of her desktop computer. Skype was up and running. The lighting was good in the room, so Erin should see her clearly. She was in her exercise clothes, and she had checked her hair and makeup in a mirror four times already. Alberto wouldn't be disturbing them, because he wasn't at home. He was with Richard, spending some time with Joshua and Shay at their house.

It was only for an hour or so, and Shay only lived a few minutes away. But Isabella was still freaking out about her little baby being without her. She tried to calm her maternal anxiety.

Even if something happens and Richard doesn't know what to do, Shay is there. You know she's a calm, capable person, and she's been a great mother to Joshua. Relax. Focus on seeing Erin. No, wait. Focus on fixing your back problem.

She rolled her eyes at herself and took a deep breath. The announcement that Erin was online came up, and Isabella reached down to the computer and clicked to video call her.

Soon, the screen filled with the image of Erin standing tall, with her hands on her hips. Isabella noted that she was in workout gear, as well, today: black, tight spandex bottoms with faded Nike logos on the thighs, and a fitted, gray tank top. Her blonde hair was pulled up in a messy bun.

"Good evenin', Ms. Writer," Erin said with a big grin.

"Hello there. It's great to see you. How's your day been?"

Erin shrugged. "Meh, same old, same old. Yours?"

"Well," she puffed out a breath. "I told my mother about the separation."

Erin grimaced. "Ouch. That sounds about as much fun as getting salt in a paper cut."

"Mm, I'd say that simile is spot on. You're starting to get to know my mother quite well."

"It's hard not to. She kinda comes up a lot."

Isabella swallowed. "I'm sorry if I bring her up too much. It must be getting tedious."

Erin held up her hands. "No, no. Shit, that's not what I meant. I just meant that she's clearly shaped you, and that she's…I don't know…the dark cloud that hangs over your life. It'd be weird if you didn't talk about her a lot. Please, don't stop sharing stuff about her. I want to know everything that happens in your life."

"All right. As long as it doesn't become repetitive."

"Nope. Not at all."

And there was that beaming Erin Black smile again. It seemed to light up the whole space between New York and Florida.

Isabella felt warm and flustered, and hurried to compose herself. "So, shall we start with the back exercises?"

"Yep. Got something to lie on this time?"

"Yes, I bought a yoga mat as you suggested. Hang on, I forgot to lay it out."

Her mental checklist had failed her. How could she forget the mat?

Because you were too busy staring at yourself in the mirror, trying to look pretty for your instructor. Vain idiot.

Isabella rolled out the dark purple mat and lay down on her back, leaning up on her elbows to look up at the computer.

Erin was fidgeting with her hair. Was she nervous? Or was she just affected by watching Isabella lying down and looking up at her like this? God, how she hoped it was the latter option.

"Nice mat! So, yeah, I can see you. I'm going to angle my laptop so you can see me on the floor too. Then you just copy me. And when you can't see me, just listen to my instructions. 'Kay?"

"Yes, that makes sense."

"Great. Let's start off with you pulling your knees up to your chest and hugging them. Then you rock from side to side. You'll be kinda rolling on your spine, easing out the muscles in your back."

Isabella watched Erin lie down and adopt the position. She looked like she was trying to roll herself into a ball. Isabella looked away from the screen and followed suit. Soon, she was rocking back and forth and had to admit that it felt good. The tense muscles seemed to be thawing from their ice-hard state. She heard a pop and winced.

"Hey, don't make that worried face. That's a good sign. Means we're getting rid of the air bubbles in the liquid in your joints and stretching parts of your back you don't naturally stretch. Now, try to roll your legs around clockwise."

Hesitantly, Isabella followed the instruction.

"Good, you've got it. Just like that. Five more."

After those five rolls, Erin said, "Looking good. Now do it counterclockwise."

Isabella tried to focus on rolling counterclockwise, but she kept thinking about Erin watching her.

Good. She's getting a view of your ass, and let's face it, that is one of your better features.

Isabella was annoyed and ashamed of the thought and willed her focus back to holding onto her legs and rocking in a circular motion. How many had she done now? Was she almost finished? This was getting difficult, and her hips protested to being stretched. There was another pop, this time from her hip joint. It felt like it relaxed after the pop, but it did nothing to cheer her up.

I'm so out of shape. I have to get back into running, even if it's just once a week. Damn, this is hard work. Okay, maybe it has to be twice a week.

"And that makes eight. Awesome. Job well done. Time to stand up," Erin chirped.

Isabella stood up. She was starting to struggle with this. Following orders and, even worse, following them from someone sounding cheerful just wasn't in her nature. It didn't help that Erin's tone was starting to remind her of Marie.

"I'm up. Now what?"

Erin grinned and winked. "Ooooh, listen to the grumpy tone on you. Don't worry, gorgeous. I'll just show you two more moves, and then you can do them whenever you want to or need to. Without me staring at you or bossing you around. Sound good?"

Isabella gave her a grateful smile and a nod. Marie certainly wouldn't have been so accommodating.

"Okay. So, first of all, let's do a normal back stretch. Reach your arms up. Then pull your stomach in a bit, and tuck your booty in at the back. Good, just like that. Aim to make yourself a straight line, and then reach for the ceiling."

Isabella imagined her fingertip getting closer to the ceiling, and soon another pop, this time from her spine, broke the silence. It came with blessed relief and made her feel like she had blood flow through parts of her back that hadn't seen any new blood since 1997.

She sneaked a glance at Erin on the screen. She looked so tall when she stretched like that. Tall, fit, and bursting with life. Isabella felt the urge to run her hands over the body on her screen. To hold Erin to her own body. She wondered what Erin smelled like. Did she wear perfume? Did someone so naturally healthy and fresh just wake up smelling of daisies and sunshine?

Erin returned to her original position. Perfect posture, hands on hips, and smile in place. "Great. Time for the last move. Stand normally, and let your hands hang down by your sides. Now just swing them from side to side. Nice and relaxed. Feel good?"

It did. Isabella's back felt more relaxed and less like any unusual movements would set it off in painful twinges. It didn't feel healed, but it was a lot less tense than it had been a few minutes ago.

Her back wasn't the only thing that felt better, though. All of her felt better. Erin's presence, even if it was just over an Internet connection, made her feel refreshed and relaxed.

Of course, it always felt good to have Erin around, but tonight it…felt different. Why was it different?

Because you're single now. There's an opportunity for a future with this woman.

She felt a thrill rush through her and had to force it down. No, no, no. She wasn't going to go down this road. Not now. She needed to get back to basics. She and Alberto were what mattered right now. When life was settled and her old relationship was a long way in the rearview mirror, then she could afford to start thinking about something new.

She saw Erin tilt her head to the side. "Hey. You okay? You look weird."

"Why thank you, Miss Black. You really know how to compliment a woman."

"Come on, you know what I meant. You okay?"

Isabella straightened up. "Yes, I'm fine. Were those all the stretches you wanted to show me?"

"Yep. Well, them and the ones I showed you last time. Do those a couple times a week, at least. If you can do them every day, then that's even better."

"I'll see what I can manage. Thank you so much. I'll have to send you a present as a kind of fee for your services."

Erin shook her head. "No need. I'm happy to help. I wanna see you anyway, and combining that with making your body feel better is great."

Isabella adjusted her hair. "I'm sending you a little something anyway, because I want to."

"Fine, I'm not gonna say no to a present, if you really want to give me one. Gonna tell me what it is?"

"No. You'll have to wait and see."

Erin poked her lower lip out. "Aw, that's not fair. Tell me."

Isabella felt laughter bubbling up. How could a grown woman look so much like a child?

"Absolutely not. You'll simply have to learn some patience."

Erin groaned. "Fine. Changing the topic, then. Let me know how you get on with the stretches. If you find they don't do the trick, I have plenty more where they came from. But I guess your back will be getting better soon, now that you'll move somewhere where you can have your own bed?"

Isabella straightened her back again, feeling how relaxed it was now. And, yes, she might have pushed her chest out a little toward the camera as she did so. "Hopefully. I'm giving that chair to charity so I won't be tempted to sleep in it anymore."

"Good. A real bed and getting that back moving will do wonders," Erin said.

"You're doing wonders." The words slipped out before Isabella had time to consider them.

"All part of the job, ma'am," Erin said with a salute.

Isabella chuckled. "You're ridiculous."

"And you love it," Erin countered.

Isabella smirked at her, refusing to answer that.

"Why don't you go get a chair and sit down? Then you can tell me about your call with your mom," Erin suggested.

And that was just what Isabella did.

They hung up more than an hour later, when Isabella got a text from Richard. He and Alberto were on their way back.

Isabella hadn't wanted to be on the phone to Erin when he got home. Even if Erin was nothing more than a friend at this point, it still felt strange to talk to her with Richard in the room. It was too close to the breakup for that.

Her eyes were drawn to the coffee table and the two books about women in comic book history. She wasn't going to mention to Erin that she had bought one for herself. She was wary of showing how invested she was in Erin's hobbies. It seemed too intimate. She'd simply send the book to Erin tomorrow and not mention anything else.

What about sending flowers too? They could perhaps be delivered on the same day as the book? No. Too romantic.

On a whim, Isabella went to the kitchen and opened the cabinet where she kept her coffee. She had ordered three packs of Azúcar Negra last time and they had arrived safely and promptly. She took one of the packets and walked back to the coffee table, putting the packet on top of the book. Erin would enjoy the luxurious beans more than flowers anyway. And it was less romantic, wasn't it? She was questioning everything now. Erin Black really had her in a spin.

The packet of Azúcar Negra left a faint smell of coffee and burnt sugar in the air. Isabella looked at her watch. There was still an hour before midnight. Supposedly too late for coffee, but what did it matter? She was free and single; she could do whatever she wanted. She walked back into the kitchen to make herself some coffee, feeling convinced that far away in New York, Erin was doing the same thing.

They would be having their pre-midnight coffee long distance...yet still together. And, for now, that was enough. But only for now.

End Book One

The story continues in
Coffee and Conclusions
(Coming January 2018)

About Emma Sterner-Radley

Having spent far too much time hopping from subject to subject at university back in her native country of Sweden, Emma finally emerged with a degree in Library and Information Science.

Now she lives with her wife and two cats in England, there is no point in saying which city as they move about once a year. She spends her free time writing, reading, daydreaming, working out, and watching whichever television show has the most lesbian subtext at the time.

Her tastes in most things usually leans towards the quirky and she loves genres like urban fantasy, magic realism, and steampunk.

Emma Sterner-Radley is also a hopeless sap for any small chubby creature with tiny legs and can often be found making heart-eyes at things like guinea pigs, Dachshunds, wombats, marmots, and human toddlers.

CONNECT WITH EMMA
Facebook: www.facebook.com/AuthorEmmaSternerRadley
Twitter: @EmmaSterner

Other Books from
Ylva Publishing

www.ylva-publishing.com

Popcorn Love

KL Hughes

ISBN: 978-3-95533-265-5
Length: 347 pages (113,000 words)

Her love life lacking, wealthy fashion exec Elena Vega agrees to a string of blind dates set up by her best friend Vivian in exchange for Vivian finding a suitable babysitter for her son, Lucas. Free-spirited college student Allison Sawyer fits the bill perfectly.

Flight SQA016

(The Flight Series – Book 1)

A.E. Radley

ISBN: 978-3-95533-447-5
Length: 303 pages (79,000 words)

Emily White works in a first-class cabin, spends a lot of time in the air and desperately misses her five-year-old son. On board she meets Olivia Lewis, who is a literal high-flying business executive with a weekly commute, a meticulous schedule, and terrible social skills.

When a personal emergency brings them together, will they be able to overcome their differences and learn how to communicate?

You're Fired

Shaya Crabtree

ISBN: 978-3-95533-754-4
Length: 193 pages (61,000 words)

When an inappropriate Secret Santa gift backfires, Rose needs her smarts to save her job, while Vivian, her sexy boss, needs her smarts to save the business. Can they stop bickering long enough to do a deal?

Shadow Haven

AJ Schippers

ISBN: 978-3-95533-845-9
Length: 322 pages (115,000 words)

A holiday on a private island comes with an erotic surprise when Julia meets the alluring Alexandra, a professional dominatrix. An explosive first meeting leads to friendship and something more sensual. Can Julia overcome her fears to explore a submissive relationship with Alexandra? What happens when power is not just left to the imagination?

Coming from Ylva Publishing

www.ylva-publishing.com

Coffee and Conclusions

(The Midnight Coffee Series — Book 2)

Emma Sterner Radley

Love brought introverted personal trainer Erin together online with writer and mother of one, Isabella. In part two of their story, their relationship blossoms as the physical distance between them shrinks. But now Erin's surfacing insecurities and Isabella's manipulative mother could tear them apart. Will their midnight coffees get them through? A lesbian romance about love finding a way.

The Music and the Mirror

Lola Keeley

Anna is the newest member of an elite ballet company. Her first class with her gifted idol, Victoria, almost ruins her career before it begins. Now Anna must face down jealousy, sabotage and injury to pour everything into opening night and prove she has what it takes to Victoria, her colleagues, and herself. In the process, Anna discovers that she and the daring, beautiful Victoria have a lot more than ballet in common, and that not every thrilling dance can be found on stage.

Long-Distance Coffee
© 2017 by Emma Sterner-Radley

ISBN: 978-3-95533-910-4

Also available as e-book.

Published by Ylva Publishing, legal entity of Ylva Verlag, e.Kfr.

Ylva Verlag, e.Kfr.
Owner: Astrid Ohletz
Am Kirschgarten 2
65830 Kriftel
Germany

www.ylva-publishing.com

First edition: 2017

Credits
Edited by Andrea Bramhall, Michelle Aguilar, and CK King
Cover Design and Print Layout by Streetlight Graphics

Printed in Great Britain
by Amazon